Praise for

THE

GREAT

GODDEN

'Rosoff's dazzling, timeless novel is a delight'
Independent

'Totally absorbing'
Press Association

'Rapture to read'
Sunday Times

'Seductive and elegant'
Observer, YA Book of the Month

'Brilliant and impactful'
Pandora Sykes

'Searingly well written'
The Times

'A wonderful, captivating writer'
Daily Telegraph

Praise for

FRIENDS LIKE THESE

'A terrific writer ... wry and spare'
Daily Mail

'This summer's must-read'
The Times

'Perfect for fans of Sally Rooney and Naoise Dolan'
Bookseller Previews

'Another utterly immersive slice of YA fiction'
Waterstones

'Effortlessly lyrical'
Stylist

'Beautifully written and evocative'
ReadingZone

'Lean, smart, sophisticated'
Spectator

ALMOST NOTHING HAPPENED

ALMOST
NOTHING
HAPPENED

MEG
ROSOFF

BLOOMSBURY
LONDON   OXFORD   NEW YORK   NEW DELHI   SYDNEY

BLOOMSBURY YA
Bloomsbury Publishing Plc
50 Bedford Square, London WC1B 3DP, UK
29 Earlsfort Terrace, Dublin 2, Ireland

BLOOMSBURY, BLOOMSBURY YA and the
Diana logo are trademarks of Bloomsbury Publishing Plc

First published in Great Britain in 2024 by Bloomsbury Publishing Plc

A catalogue record for this book is available from the British Library

ISBN: HB: 978-1-5266-4618-7; TPB: 978-1-5266-4619-4;
eBook: 978-1-5266-4615-6; ePDF: 978-1-5266-4614-9

2 4 6 8 10 9 7 5 3 1

Typeset by RefineCatch Limited, Bungay, Suffolk

Printed and bound in Great Britain by CPI Group (UK) Ltd, Croydon CR0 4YY

MIX
Paper | Supporting
responsible forestry
FSC
www.fsc.org FSC® C171272

To find out more about our authors and books visit www.bloomsbury.com
and sign up for our newsletters

1

Eurostar was showing a twenty-minute delay, which was perfect because if I didn't get something to eat before I boarded the train I'd have to eat my own liver.

I joined the queue for a sandwich with my mate, Moe, and texted home that we were running late. They were picking me up at St Pancras and might want to leave later.

Immediately the text went through, my phone rang.

Dad.

Moe clocked my expression and raised an eyebrow. It was incredibly noisy in the terminal, but he could see something was up.

I let it go to voicemail. Whatever it was, I didn't want to hear.

My dad knows I can't stand talking on the phone, so a phone call must be something completely urgent, like MI6 just got in touch to say there's a bomb on your train. If that were the case, I figured he'd follow up with a text.

Maybe I was overreacting. I stared at the phone, wishing technology had advanced enough to send a precis of whatever topic the person on the other end was planning to raise. It would be good for avoiding break-up calls, or rejections of any sort. Moe once told me that all bad news comes by text, so maybe I shouldn't have worried.

We squeezed on to a low table between seats to eat our sandwiches in peace, an impossibility given Moe is six-foot-two and we were surrounded by the whole European Adventures Abroad team all muttering into headsets like they were running security for Taylor Swift. Just now, they were distributing UK passports to the younger kids, threatening that if anyone lost theirs, they'd have to stay in France forever. Some of the kids seemed to consider this a good thing. I guess you never know what's going on in someone else's family.

My phone rang again. I ignored it with mounting dread. What was so important that he had to talk to me before I got on the train?

I was prepared for bad news thanks to extensive life experience. And although I made light of my depressing summer because what else can you do when kids your own age are risking death crossing the Channel on inflatable bath toys, still, it was dispiriting. Not that I felt sorry for myself in the wider scheme of things, I'd just hoped it might have gone better.

My phone rang again. Oh God. No way!

Three calls in ten minutes? Someone had definitely died. Or maybe my parents were getting divorced and he wanted to break it to me slowly – he'd tell me in

France that they weren't getting along too well, and by the time I got to London, Dad would be running off with a girl my age or Mum wanted an open marriage. Or maybe he'd taken that job in Dubai (what job in Dubai?), where the temperature made life impossible and drinking was punishable by flogging. Or wait. Could Mum be pregnant? At fifty-six? Please God, no.

I knew this sort of thing would happen if I let them out of my sight for a whole summer, but honestly, I cannot keep watch over the elderly twenty-four hours a day. Do you have any idea how depressing it is not to trust your parents to act normal for one short month?

Shit. Shit. Shit. I switched the phone off and dropped it in my pocket.

Moe looked at me. 'Do not seek misfortune,' he intoned, quoting his Tai Chi master. 'It will find you in its time.' And then he smiled beatifically.

'So, if my Dad's planning to take a job in Dubai and sign us up for an international school famous for

4

the execution of homosexuals, I should just chill because I'll get the news eventually?'

'Live, laugh, love.'

'I can't live-laugh-love if I'm being stoned to death.'

Moe frowned. 'You're not gay, are you?'

'Not at the moment.'

Moe was off again. 'Knowledge speaks. Wisdom listens.'

'And anyway, you are. What if you want to come visit me?'

'Not happening. Don't cry because it's over. Smile because it happened.'

'How have I lived without your crappy wisdom all summer? Let's go to Duty Free.'

'For what?'

'Distraction.'

I took the last bite of my sandwich and tried to reckon with the weird feeling in my head. Suddenly I couldn't chew because I couldn't catch my breath and my jaw ached and I was pretty sure I was having a heart attack. Oh Lord, breathe, breathe. I was going to suffocate any second. Shit. A panic attack. Why now, particularly? Though panic attacks often hit me in airports and train stations. Maybe it was the word 'terminal' that set them off.

Moe stared at his phone, oblivious. Was there a bag I could breathe into? Was there a friend I could depend on?

We got to Duty Free, me sweating, swaying, unable to catch my breath.

Moe drifted over to perfume to douse himself in Chanel No. 5.

Would they let me buy a bottle of vodka if I claimed a medical emergency?

Bonjour mesdames et messieurs, l'Eurostar numéro neuf zero trente-et-un, départ à 13:12 à destination de Londres St Pancras, est prêt pour l'embarquement, voie six.

Across the waiting area, EAA camp counsellors

with CIA headsets had started to corral everyone on to the train. Checking for bags left behind.

'You OK, man?' Moe looked concerned at last. He smelled like Marilyn Monroe.

I told him I needed the toilet and he said he'd meet me on board.

What a car-crash of a summer. And how appropriate for it to end in a full-blown outbreak of existential distress.

I moved like a zombie towards the toilets, locked myself in a cubicle and dropped my head between my knees. My heart clanged in my ears. Oh God oh God oh God. Make it stop.

Breathe. Breathe. Breathe.

Time passed. The waves of nausea began to subside. I heard another announcement.

Attention please, Eurostar number 9031 to London will depart from platform six in ten minutes. If you are in possession of a ticket, please board the train immediately.

Ten minutes? Oh Christ. I lurched to my feet and ran back to the gate, where the last few stragglers were hurrying down the ramp. I arrived just as the bored train attendant reached to clip a rope firmly across the entrance.

'*Allez vite. Dépêchez-vous.*' She imbued the words with the same urgency she might have used to say, 'Nice hat, Grandma.'

I stopped. Stared. At her. At the rope. At the train below on the platform. At all the happy returning language students exchanging stories of brilliant achievements and memories that would last a lifetime.

And then I hitched my backpack over my shoulder and reversed my trajectory. At the bottom of the ramp, I could just about see Moe gesticulating wildly, saw him drop his arms in astonishment as I turned away from the ramp, away from the train, away from the boarding gate, away from the waiting area, away from customs, away from my miserable summer, away from whatever new challenge my parents had planned for my welcome home ceremony, away from everything I couldn't stand about my life and myself, down the stairs, away from Gare du Nord and out on to the streets of Paris.

Behind me, the train pulled out of the station.

Ping. A text from Moe.

'What the hell, man? What happened?'

Almost nothing happened. That was the point.

2

I didn't have the time of my life on my French exchange. I didn't learn fluent French. I didn't develop a passion for French culture or cuisine. I didn't make lifelong friends. I didn't lose my virginity.

What did I do? I worried. Sulked. Fell in love with a girl who cared nothing for me. Avoided human contact, pretended to be bored. Took interminable walks with the family dog – a small hairy mutt who liked me about half as much as I liked him.

It was not my finest hour. Not that I blamed France.

It all started with me asking the best student in

class to write an introductory letter to my French family. Mediocre language skills had made my own letter *indéchiffrable*. Indecipherable.

This was, of course, cheating, but it did teach me a valuable life lesson, one you might want to take on board for your own future: faking a foreign language is not sustainable over time.

The photo I enclosed with the (outsourced) letter captured my best angle and unaccountably made me look almost cool, when in real life I was anything but. And compared to Florian and Élodie (my glamorous teen counterparts), I was about as glamorous as a chip butty.

They greeted me with a gentle torrent of French, the usual sort of 'Hello, how are you, we're so pleased to meet you, we hope your trip was pleasant', etc. etc., and I greeted them back with a few stumbled phrases that I tried to imbue with gratitude and goodwill. But it felt as if I'd been struck by lightning and somehow couldn't remember even basic

Year 7 French, the '*Bonjour Madame Thibault, bonjour Monsieur Thibault*' level that guaranteed you'd be able to ask with confidence if the croissant was gluten-free.

I did my best to keep up my side of the relationship, but had to admit I knew nothing about jazz, with which Florian and Élodie were obsessed, or sex (ditto), or French literature or politics. Their tiny town in south-west France hosted a world-famous early music festival every year, and much time was spent discussing the virtues of Monteverdi vs Handel; at least, that's what I think they were discussing, it was hard to tell. Another conversational blind spot.

Once the dynamic settled, I tried to make myself invisible – hanging back with a book until everyone had gone out and then having breakfast by myself in an empty apartment and slithering out *avec le chien*, Titou, for a walk in the quiet countryside. I simply didn't have the confidence to speak French and try to improve, which kind of defeated the whole exercise.

Don't roll your eyes, I couldn't help it. Maybe you don't remember a time when you barely had the confidence to ask where the toilet was. Maybe you were never that insecure. If so, congratulations. I envy you still.

I tried being easy to have around. I worked really hard at it. What is it that people want to feel when they meet you? Does he laugh at my jokes? Is he *sympathique*? Sparky? What team does he support? But in the case of me in France, I didn't speak, so how would they know?

During the first week, the beautiful Élodie invited me to a picnic at some gloriously handsome young man's grand home where a select group of beautiful, educated young French people talked (too fast and in incomprehensible slang) about – presumably – cinema, politics, music, literature and sex, while I gazed off into space trying desperately to look as if I might be thinking about something amusing. It was agony.

Titou was a pretty good companion, once I got

my head around the fact that not all dogs spoke English. He had a passion for hunting rats along the edge of the vineyards where the grapes were just starting to ripen. This made our walks a lot more interesting. I learned to shout '*Viens ici!*' when he strayed too far away and '*Laisse!*' when he showed signs of eating the rat he'd caught. Sometimes his battle with a rodent lasted longer than I was strictly happy to watch, sometimes the squeaking was awful to listen to, and usually I found myself sympathising with the rat. My French family clearly thought Titou and I were intellectually compatible, though I'm pretty sure he was smarter.

Luckily, I'd brought along *Crime and Punishment*, because Moe said it was a laugh, which, strictly speaking, it wasn't, though even I had to acknowledge that Raskolnikov's existence was marginally worse than mine, which helped. Particularly once he was sentenced to eight years hard labour in Siberia.

On the first day, dinner was a stilted affair of everyone talking around and over me, me entirely failing to get the hang of sophisticated phrases like 'Please pass the butter', and the specified goal of strengthening international relationships falling very flat. What, in short, is more boring than a charmless foreigner, too nervous to take the risk of speaking, plonked into a middle-class family whose earnest politesse barely conceals the wish that he wasn't there?

In short? Nothing.

3

For breakfast, my French family ate pieces of a flat dinner-plate shaped cake they referred to merely as 'galette'. It tasted mainly of butter, and though indescribably delicious on the day it was bought (fresh and slightly bendy), it tasted better and better as days passed and it turned stale.

Galette was just about my favourite thing about France. Obviously, I loved Élodie, but I didn't feel the same futile desperation to make a good impression on galette. On my last day, I walked down to the bakery and bought two to take home, each beautifully wrapped in cellophane and tied with a small piece of striped ribbon. I didn't love all French specialities – horse burgers caused unease – but I did appreciate the way they packaged patisserie: printed papers, white boxes, ribbon, like everything you ate was a gift.

At least I'll have emergency sustenance for the day, I thought, having abandoned my seat on Eurostar and set off for my unknown future in Paris without fully considering that I was fatally short of money for luxuries like food, transport and shelter. I had no money, in fact, except a few coins and an emergency credit card for use in emergencies only, which had been impressed upon me so often and at such length that I hadn't dared touch it all summer.

I considered declaring an emergency, but it wasn't even one thirty. Maybe I'd wait till five.

I did have an ace in the hole, namely my cousin Harrison, who'd been studying music in France for the past seven years and whose details I had on my phone just in case I needed a matching kidney donor over the summer.

He would of course love to see me (so I'd been told), even though he probably had no idea who I was, not having laid eyes on me since I was four. I didn't think I'd recognise him at all. We didn't spend a lot of time with his side of the family, as we lived south of the Thames and they lived in Sheffield.

I turned my phone on, shot a text off to Harrison telling him I was unexpectedly coming to visit. Wouldn't he be surprised when I showed up at his door! Wouldn't I be surprised if he was right now playing a concert tour in Amsterdam or Egypt?

I could hear Moe's words murmuring gently in the ether all around me.

'Destiny will guide your feet.'

'The journey is the destination.'

'The path to wisdom begins with a single step.'

And so on and bloody on.

Conserving battery, I shut my phone off again. Also, the number of people I didn't want to talk to kept growing.

Harrison lived near Bastille, a forty-five-minute walk from Gare du Nord according to Maps, so I set off. It was hot. Pretty much unbearably hot. Visible waves of heat rose from the pavements. The streets of Paris seemed quiet for such a big city, even the cafés were deserted. It was too hot to sit outside, too hot to drink coffee. Too hot, even, to drink *citron pressé* or eat a *croque monsieur* under an umbrella. In what everyone said was the worst heatwave since the ice age, anyplace that wasn't air-conditioned wasn't possible.

The long walk should have been an opportunity to immerse myself in the world's most graceful city, the quaint streets and elegant shops, the stylish denizens, their beautiful children and coiffured pets. But the streets were empty, and with no water supply, I couldn't contemplate anything except how thirsty I was. The breeze, such as it was, blew hot as a dragon's breath and was worse than no breeze at all.

And yet, something about bolting had eased my

feelings of panic, despite a vague sense that what I'd done was rash and completely fantastical; after all, there was no evidence that we were moving to Dubai except that my father worked for an oil company and often travelled to that part of the world. My parents had been arguing about it a lot this year, Mum shouting, 'Why don't you quit?' and Dad answering, 'Who do you think pays for this lifestyle?'

In our house, the climate crisis was personal.

'This lifestyle' was funded by Dad and my GP mother, in a determinedly middle-class suburb of South London with decent local schools, and the occasional holiday somewhere like Scotland or Devon. My two siblings and I never had to choose between shoes and food. We knew we were lucky because everyone told us all the time.

About a year ago, my father had been offered a job in Dubai and laughed it off, saying, 'I'm not quite that desperate yet.'

But maybe he was now? Maybe inflation had

increased the cost of our lifestyle and he was doing it for us? I had no real idea how lifestyles worked.

Walking and sweating, sweating and walking, the heat weighed me down so much that I stopped at a large public bin, opened my backpack and jettisoned everything I could live without. Socks, sweatshirt, books, shampoo … amazing what seemed unnecessary when you had to carry it in a heatwave.

Eventually I found Harrison's street, the house number and flat number, and pressed the buzzer. Waited. Buzzed again.

No answer.

There was nothing to do but sit on a step opposite, in the shade, where I could observe without being mistaken for a runaway summer exchange student. People came and people went, and none looked remotely like my cousin Harrison, or what I vaguely imagined he should look like.

Just before four, I buzzed again, in case Harrison had moved and I had to beg whoever had recently rented his flat to let me sleep on the sofa for a night or two.

I had no plan B.

But miracle of miracles, a disembodied crackly voice called, '*Allo, bonjour? Allo? C'est qui?*'

'Harrison?'

'*Oui?* Yes? Callum?'

'Oh, thank goodness you're there. Please can I come up? I'm in kind of a predicament.'

The door buzzed and I trudged to the third floor with wet armpits and a pounding heart, hoping a number of diverse hopes, mainly that Harrison had a strong belief in the value of family ties.

He peered at me as I came through the door and I peered back.

'Harrison?'

'Callum?'

'Yes, hello, thank you for answering the door.'

'Well, hello. I got your text. To be honest, I didn't

really expect you to visit, though your mum told my mum you might. Come in.'

I shrugged off my near-empty backpack and placed it in the corner so he wouldn't trip over it. The flat was tiny.

'Sit down. Can I get you a cold drink?' Harrison seemed tense.

'Just a glass of water please.' Make that a bucket with ice. It was fiendishly hot in his flat. 'I'm sorry just to show up, did I interrupt something? Do you have to be somewhere?'

'It's fine,' he called from the rabbit-hutch-sized kitchen. 'I was just practising. There's a lot happening today. You didn't buzz before, did you? I never hear the bell when I'm making a racket.'

I shook my head and accepted the water. 'You play the clarinet?' I could see an instrument lying across a chair but didn't quite recognise it.

'Oboe.'

'Oboe,' I echoed. Of course.

23

'You've been on a French exchange?' When I nodded, he asked, 'How was it?'

'Awful. My fault not theirs. They were nice and gorgeous and polite, but my French was terrible and they thought I was a moron.'

'But … you improved over the summer? Isn't that sort of the point?'

If only he knew. 'Not really. I got off to a terrible start and never recovered.'

I could have told Harrison that within ten minutes of arriving at my new French home, I'd encountered a foot-long poo floating in the toilet, which pretty much set the tone for the rest of the summer. But I didn't. Anyway, strictly speaking that wasn't the bad start, that was just an *amuse-bouche* for what was to come.

'Ah well.' He nodded sympathetically. 'The French can be superior bastards, I mostly hate them. Wait, that's not true, I really like some of them. My girl-friend's French. She's incredibly superior, which is why I like her. Liked her. She's my ex-girlfriend now. Probably nothing to do with being French.' He sighed. 'It's hard to generalise about sixty-seven million people. Come to think of it, I mostly hate the English too.'

I agreed that it was hard to generalise and though I wouldn't go so far as hating all sixty-seven million British, there were definitely a fair few I could do without. And actually, I'd been incredibly partial to one or two French people over the summer. One, in fact. But more of that later.

'Hello?'

Harrison was staring at me.

'Sorry. So, I guess you're dying to know what I'm doing here.'

Harrison frowned. 'Not really. You had a spare half-hour after visiting the Louvre?'

'I'm supposed to be on a Eurostar back to London,' I said. 'I did a runner.'

'A runner?' He blinked. 'Why?'

'I don't know.' I realised now that I didn't. 'I had three suspicious phone calls in a row from my father, and I have pretty good instincts for bad news, which I felt certain this was, and it brought on a panic attack, and I couldn't breathe, and the thought of being on a train seemed impossible under the circumstances, so in the end I just … didn't go.'

'What was the news?'

'What news?'

'What was the bad news your dad was phoning to tell you?'

Oh. 'I don't know. I turned my phone off.'

'Wow,' Harrison said. 'That's quite …'

'Conflict averse? I know. Everyone says I need to get hold of myself. Face up to life.' I shrugged. 'Look, I don't suppose you'd let me crash here for a couple of nights?'

Harrison shifted uncomfortably. 'Oh God, no, it's really not … I mean, no, probably not … In short, no.'

'I swear to God I won't cramp your style and I'm perfectly happy sleeping on the floor and I'll get my own food, and if your ex-girlfriend comes back I'll just go out and walk around the neighbourhood. I normally wouldn't ask but as you can see, it's kind of an emergency and I don't know anyone else in Paris.'

'Couldn't you go home? Won't your parents be frantic? Have you told them where you are?'

I hadn't. And let's face it, I couldn't. Not just yet. 'Kind of,' I said, hoping he'd be too polite to ask what that meant.

'Look, Callum, I'm sure you're perfectly harmless, but I have a concert tonight and a rehearsal in half an hour and I don't like other people very much and it's hot – your timing isn't exactly – how can I put this nicely—'

'Could I come?'

'To the rehearsal?'

'The concert.'

He frowned again. 'You're interested in classical music?'

No. 'Very much so,' I said. 'I'd really like to hear you play. And if I can just stay for a couple of days, I'll leave you in peace and you'll never have to see me again.'

'It's not that I don't want ever to have to see you again.' Being cornered was affecting his grammar. 'It's just not the best, not the most convenient …' He sighed, deeply. 'OK, fine. But only two nights. You can sleep on the couch. I have to go now; I'll text you the address and leave a ticket at the box office.' He looked at me with an air of resignation. 'Can you stay out of trouble please and not go through my stuff?'

I nodded.

'And if your parents call, asking whether I've had any contact and do I know if you've been kidnapped and murdered?'

I fidgeted. 'Could you possibly not answer their calls for a day or two – so you don't have to lie?'

'Please tell me you have a plan.'

'Yes, of course,' I lied. 'I don't have the money to live in Paris for the rest of my life and, as I might have mentioned, my French isn't up to much.'

I smiled a sad little smile that said I was incredibly grateful to him for indulging me and my panic attack and my bad French and my certainty that my dad had been calling with news about my future in Dubai. It also communicated that he wouldn't get done for abduction, probably just for harbouring a runaway teen, which carried a much shorter jail sentence.

Harrison smiled back, in the most half-hearted way imaginable, a way that said he wished I hadn't come into his life at all, but particularly not tonight, and he hoped I would soon be gone and not his responsibility, and though he supposed he'd have to be friendly if we ever met again, it wouldn't be a meeting he hoped would take place any time soon.

'Thank you, Harrison, thank you from the

bottom of my heart. Go to your rehearsal. I'll be fine here and come home with you after the concert, so you don't even need to leave a key.'

So off he set with his oboe packed away in a chestnut leather case, looking dubious in the extreme (Harrison, not the oboe) and texting me the address of the concert hall ('It's not far, you can walk'). I thanked him again for saving my life, and when he left, I sat down on the couch, relieved and sweating and thankful to know what the next twenty-four hours looked like.

I breathed a sigh of relief worthy of a man with a temporary stay of execution.

4

The first time I met Florian, I thought he looked like a younger, less goofy Ryan Gosling – same endearing puppy-dog eyes, same floppy blond hair. In fact he looked like a younger, less goofy, not at all friendly Ryan Gosling, but I hoped that was just a first impression. Perhaps he was a book you couldn't judge from its cover.

I had to share a room with him, which didn't make anyone happy, but we kept such incompatible hours that we hardly ever overlapped when fully conscious. You could see he wanted nothing to do with me, nothing to do with this whole French exchange malarkey, just a nice quiet summer having

31

lots of sex with his girlfriend. I couldn't really blame him.

Our average conversation went like this:

HIM: *Ça va?*
ME: *Oui, ça va.*

Or sometimes:

HIM: *Ça va?*
ME: *Ça va bien. Et toi?*

We always stopped just short of exploring the meaning of life.

After dinner each night, I retired with Raskolnikov or a podcast, while Florian and Élodie went out to the festival with friends. There were classical and jazz concerts every night at the Benedictine abbey, and all the kids who helped with ushering, ticket sales or stacking chairs got in free. Locally, it was the event of the year and pretty much everyone between fourteen and twenty turned out to volunteer in hopes of meeting exotic foreigners. They also seemed to like the music. Performers and music lovers from all over the region came, and from Europe, and the world.

I tagged along for the first couple of times, and the concerts were fine, but I hated not being able to participate socially. After the first few days, Élodie and Florian asked politely if I wanted to come along while not really wanting me to, and I just as politely declined until the precedent was set in stone. After about ten days, they no longer asked, and I could no longer change my mind.

Mme Lemoine was nothing like most of the English mothers I knew, including my mother, who styled herself to heighten a glancing resemblance to Kate Winslet. All the mothers in my orbit wore jeans, trainers and ponytails and drank flat whites out of cardboard cups. Most of them worked as teachers, or in marketing or the NHS. But Mme Lemoine looked like a middle-aged woman from another era – always carefully coiffed and neatly dressed in a flowered frock that fell just to the knee. She didn't work and was kind to me, initiated simple conversations about current events and took me on errands long after everyone else had kicked me into the long grass.

Monsieur Lemoine made himself scarce during the day. They'd explained what he did for a living, but of course I only half grasped it. Was he a lawyer or an avocado importer? Did he work for the railway? Or merely take a train to work? My partial take-out from every sentence led to endless misunderstandings.

And then there was Élodie.

Would I ever be able to think of Élodie without an agonising mix of longing and despair? Everything about her turned me inside out. Glossy hair. Large intelligent eyes. No make-up. Direct gaze. Frequent

smile. She held out her hand when we were introduced, met my gaze and murmured, '*Enchantée*,'
with a slightly ironical inflection, at which point my
heart left my chest, crawled over to the gutter, and
lay there, flapping.

I literally could not speak in her presence. Was it
possible to spend weeks in a not very big flat with a
girl like that and not make a complete fool of myself?

Rhetorical.

But forgive me if I don't feel like going over all that
just now.

Mme Lemoine disapproved of Élodie. She didn't
make enough of an effort. With a daughter that
lovely, *Maman* wanted make-up, dresses, high heels.
She wanted suitors with money and position, a serious campaign to marry well. What else was the
point of a beautiful daughter?

But Élodie fancied herself an intellectual, read
Flaubert and flirted, liked to dance, found money
boring unless it was being spent on her. I convinced

myself that she was unorthodox, that she might like me because I was everything inappropriate, or as I liked to think, singular.

'*Ah*,' she said, when she saw what I was reading. '*Dostoevsky. Super!*'

'*Super*' was not the word I'd have chosen for the greatest literary depressive of all time. Was she being ironic? Or was there a nuance I'd missed? I ran it over in my head, imagined her coming to London with seven volumes of Proust and me saying 'Super!' in a way that meant, 'Well, aren't *you* the literary sophisticate …'

Are you beginning to grasp my problem? It wasn't just the grammar that tripped me up, but the subtleties of language, the inflections, inferences. Knowing the meaning of a word was only the beginning. Was '*super*' nice-ironic? Not-very-nice-sarcastic? How was a person to know?

Breathe, I told myself. The past is past.

Foraging around in Harrison's tiny fridge, I found

a few beers and some lettuce from a past decade, so I cracked open one of the galettes and washed it down with a beer. Then I had a cold shower, pulled out the only clean T-shirt I'd kept and combed my hair. I was way overdue for a haircut, so I found some scissors and tried to cut straight lines where things stuck out worst. I wouldn't say it improved things, but from some angles I looked OK. At 18:30, I pulled the door shut behind me, ran down the stairs and stepped out into the heavy evening.

5

As Harrison had promised, it took ten minutes to get to the concert hall and I arrived sweating. My ticket was waiting at the box office and I managed to ask for it in French. They didn't answer in English, which always felt like a triumph.

The place wasn't air-conditioned, which meant attendance was sparse, mostly people in their twenties and thirties. I'd always assumed you had to be old to like classical music, but this had proved untrue in France. I guessed most of the audience members were musicians, music students or friends of the performers – who else felt compelled to go to a concert on a night this hot?

They'd run out of programmes by the time I arrived, which was fine, as none of the composers' names meant much to me. Bach. I'd heard of him, but could I even identify the sound of an oboe? Probably not. When the lights went down and the murmuring stopped, I gave myself over gratefully to the atmosphere of order and calm. Behind us, fans hummed softly and my damp neck caught the hint of a breeze. Even without the music it was a nice end to a stressful day.

The guy next to me turned out to be some sort of afficionado, totally immersed in the music. He swayed, tapped his fingers and even hummed faintly, as if he couldn't contain himself. At the interval he turned to me with sharp glittering eyes and said, '*C'était incroyable, non!?*'

'*Incroyable*,' I agreed, but with one word he somehow clocked that I was not a native speaker and switched languages.

'English?' He asked. 'American?'

'English.' He was good-looking in a dishevelled sort of way, the impression amplified by a somewhat nervous demeanour. I told him that Harrison Laine was my cousin and had given me the ticket, that I didn't know much about classical music, but it sounded nice.

'Nice?' The guy frowned, shook his head. 'I am also a musician and I can tell you that "nice" is an insult to music like this. You happen to be related to a very great *joueur de hautbois*. Harrison Laine plays with rare skill and feeling. Are you staying with him? Visiting Paris?'

I was surprised to find myself in conversation with a stranger, but it felt OK, like I'd hurled myself out into the world and the world hadn't spat me out. In a mixture of French and English I explained about abandoning my group and Eurostar, and not wanting to go back to London.

He frowned. '*Tu es en cavale?* An escapee? Like in the war movies? Not the greatest time to be in Paris, there's a curfew to keep looters from going crazy in the heat. The streets are abandoned, *tu vois*? People over sixty have been warned to stay home, that's why this place isn't full. But I'm pleased to meet you. I'm Arnaud.' He spoke quickly. The more I looked at him, the more jittery he appeared.

'Callum,' I said, and we shook hands.

'Callum, great name.' He turned to the woman beside him. 'Lilou, this is Callum. Harrison Laine's cousin.'

'*Ciao*,' said Lilou with a smile. She wore white jeans, a cream-coloured sleeveless shirt and black boots. Despite the heat, she carried a leather jacket. Was she his girlfriend?

'*Ciao*, Lilou,' I said. Why did French women have such gorgeous names? You never met one called Elsa or Mags.

Lilou, I thought. *Élodie*.

People squeezed past us to get back to their seats, tripping over Arnaud's bag, as the warning bell rang for part two. The emotional stress of the day and the heat caught up with me all at once and with the music tripping along pleasantly, I dozed off.

Rapturous applause woke me. Arnaud was on his feet along with most of the rest of the audience, and then the musicians took their places and played a sparkling little encore, the musical equivalent of a pink macaron. Afterwards Harrison bowed repeatedly and left the stage, the lights came up and everyone began to file out.

I was bleary and blinking, and Arnaud looked at me critically. 'Some fan.'

'Leave him,' Lilou said. And then to me, 'It's hard to do anything in this heat.'

'*Il fait chaud* for sure,' I quipped, like an idiot.

Lilou smiled. 'Are you going backstage to see your cousin?'

'Is that what you're supposed to do?' I had no idea.

'Yes, we'll take you and you can introduce us.'

'It will be fantastic to meet the great Harrison

Laine.' Arnaud shook his head. 'And you turning out to be his cousin. *Incroyable!*'

There was something about Arnaud that made me uncomfortable. I couldn't put my finger on it, something not quite right. 'Dog instinct disorder' Moe called it, when you sniffed a person or situation and it smelled off.

We went around to the back of the stage, through the curtains where people were milling about, then down a corridor to a cramped room full of musicians all changing clothes and packing up their instruments and bidding their friends goodbye in a mishmash of languages.

Harrison had his back to me, and I approached diffidently.

'Harrison? You were amazing,' I said. 'I had no idea you were so famous.' Shit. Famous. Wrong word.

Arnaud rolled his eyes. I really hoped he didn't plan to shop me to my relative, who absolutely did

43

not need to know that I'd slept through most of the concert.

'Did you really like it?' Harrison asked. 'The Albinoni is a nightmare to play. Who'd have guessed you'd turn out to be a classical music lover.'

Arnaud kept quiet and I was confused by how my opinion seemed to matter to Harrison, when I was the very definition of an opinion that didn't matter. I think I'd slept through the Albinoni but vowed to google it later.

'Harrison, this is Arnaud and Lilou. I sat next to them. Arnaud is also a musician. They're big fans.'

Arnaud stared intently at Harrison. 'Fantastic concert, *tellement exceptionnel*. I am only an amateur. But the Bach, such beautiful playing, it brought me to tears.'

Lilou simply smiled and said, '*Bravo*.'

Arnaud switched to French and he and Harrison chatted for a few minutes, then he indicated the door.

'We'll wait for you in the lobby, Harrison, and then you'll stay for a drink?'

'Everyone's going to Le Canard,' Harrison said. 'It's air-conditioned. We can meet there. I won't be long.'

Arnaud led, and I walked beside Lilou to the bar.

'Look,' she said, indicating people emerging on to the street. 'The heatwave is meant to last a week. When it's this hot, people sleep all day and come out at night when it's cooler. *Comme les blaireaux.*'

Blaireaux? Bats? Hedgehogs? Leopards?

We arrived at a busy bar just down the street with a large oil painting of a duck at the entrance. The air conditioning meant it was jammed and you could hear the mechanism groaning somewhere in the back, clacking and grinding in its attempt to keep the place cool. People had pulled tables together and were sitting in groups, Arnaud ordered wine, Harrison arrived and bought another bottle, and soon I was feeling pretty happy, more than a bit drunk and speaking French better than I thought possible. Harrison warned me to be careful, that the heat caused dehydration which magnified the effects of alcohol.

After everything that's happened today, I thought, bring it on.

Lilou didn't sit next to Arnaud. She pulled up a chair next to me instead, asking lots of questions about my summer, which improved somewhat in the telling thanks to the wine and some slightly embellished anecdotes. There were whole areas I couldn't yet find humour in.

Over the next hour, we talked, in an improvised franglais. I told her about my hosts and my failure to learn French properly. She corrected my more egregious grammatical errors, and expressed disapproval when I told her about Florian and his girlfriend, Jacqui.

'They had sex in the next bed when they thought you were asleep? That is appalling, and they call themselves hosts? You had a terrible family, that was your only problem. It wasn't your fault at all. I am embarrassed for all French people.'

It was nice of her to say.

'And Élodie? Was she nice to you?'

I wasn't about to tell her about Élodie and how much I loved her. It was too humiliating. 'She was OK,' I stuttered. 'Very beautiful.'

Lilou narrowed her eyes. 'You were in love with her?'

Rumbled.

'And she? Not interested in you?'

Ditto.

Lilou shook her head. 'She sounds like a bitch.'

'No, no, not at all.'

Lilou snorted. 'Take my word for it.'

Kind thought, but she obviously failed to understand that the default position of the female world was not to fall in love with me. 'It was my fault. My French was so bad I had the smartest girl in class write my introduction letter to the family …'

'Well, that was a mistake,' she said. 'Next time write your own letter.'

'I know.' I hung my head. The thought of the fake letter still filled me with shame. 'I'm a terrible person.'

She frowned. 'Did you strangle a baby? Burn down a hospital? *Non?* Perspective, Callum, please. You and your family were a bad match. *C'est tout.* And by the way, your French is not so bad.'

It hadn't occurred to me that fault for the miserable summer might not be all mine. This possibility required cognitive revision on a grand scale. And as for my French, 'not so bad' was high praise. Praise combined with wine – such undeserved bliss!

I needed to change the subject. 'And you, Lilou – what do you do?'

'I work for a lobbying group. An environmental NGO, like Greenpeace.'

Oh God. 'My father works for an oil company.'

She executed a classic French moue, halfway

between a shrug and a dismissal. 'So? It's his job not yours. When you get a job, you will do something better.'

End of subject.

I was on my fourth glass of wine. 'Is Arnaud your boyfriend?'

Lilou laughed. 'Arnaud? God help me. He's my stepbrother. His mother married my father. I've known him since I was ten.'

Excellent news. I wondered how old she was. It was hard to tell, and I couldn't measure her against the girls I'd met over the past month. With their pretty clothes and provincial manners, Élodie's friends seemed like a different species, somehow older and younger at the same time. Lilou told me she was born in Paris, had lived here all her life, but she wasn't what I expected of the typical Parisienne.

The typical Parisienne! What a ridiculous idea. I'd laugh for a week if someone tried to tell me about the typical Londoner.

What had I imagined? Someone perfectly groomed, perfectly styled, perfectly feminine and perfectly confident. Lilou was not that person. She seemed tough, sensible and smart. Down to earth. Urban. I would not have called her feminine exactly, though she was attractive. As for the black boots and leather jacket on a night this hot, I didn't understand it, but what did I know about fashion? She was nice to me, and that was practically the best thing about her.

Across the table, Harrison and Arnaud sat close together and talked intently, and I wondered if all this was about the concert, or perhaps they'd discovered some other passion they had in common. Arnaud appeared to be doing most of the talking and Harrison was listening intently, occasionally nodding. Lilou kept glancing at Arnaud while he avoided looking at her. I couldn't figure out the agenda. She seemed to be waiting for something from him and he seemed to be pretending she wasn't.

'Arnaud!' She eventually called across the table to him. '*On doit parler de quelque chose, tu sais?*' Something to discuss. She wasn't exactly informing him. It came across as a warning more than anything.

'*Oui, oui, bien sûr,*' he called back. But when Lilou went off to the toilet some time later, Arnaud stood up, tapped his credit card on the payment machine, embraced Harrison like a long-lost friend, picked up his bag and left.

'Say goodbye to Lilou for me,' he called from the door. 'Tell her I'll be in touch.'

When Lilou returned to find him gone, she was furious.

'*Salaud!*' she swore, stamped her foot, and then grabbed her jacket and raced out the door without even a glance back at me.

Harrison asked if I was ready to go and reached down for his oboe case, which he'd kept safely at his feet all night. But something was wrong. He lifted

51

the leather case as if its weight confused him and carefully opened the clasp. Then turned it to show me the interior.

Empty.

'My God.' He looked stricken.

'But what ...' I couldn't even think of a question to ask. 'Could it have dropped out?' Could your oboe have undone the clasp from the inside of the case, wiggled out of its deep velvet indentations and rolled away across the floor of the café, out the door and down the street?

Why yes, Callum. That seems likely.

Time slowed. Harrison didn't move.

The circle of shock gradually expanded through the restaurant and all the musicians began to talk at once, converging on Harrison like worried ducks. I heard murmurs of 'What's happened?' in French and English, and a few close friends rushed to Harrison's side, stared at the empty case, checked under the table (as if it might be rolling around unnoticed at our feet). They asked the most obvious questions ('Did you forget it? Have you picked up the wrong case?') while Harrison stood still as stone, staring straight ahead, expressionless.

'Someone's taken it,' he said mechanically. 'I must inform the police.'

Around us, musicians were murmuring about reports of musical instrument thefts through the ages. It was not unknown, they were saying, although equally, oboes were not commonly targeted. And no one had seen anything out of the ordinary tonight.

Excuse my genuine naivety, but why would anyone steal an oboe? Wouldn't a Stradivarius make more sense? And how could the hypothetical thief insinuate his- or herself next to Harrison for long enough to remove the oboe from its case under the table without arousing suspicion?

Unless the thief was Arnaud.

Harrison must have come to the same conclusion.

We both looked round to where Lilou had been sitting a minute earlier.

Arnaud and Lilou.

Not boyfriend and girlfriend. Stepbrother and sister. And partners in crime? Less than compatible ones, it seemed, based on her reaction to his disappearance. Perhaps she was expecting him to wait for her. Perhaps she had planned to drive the getaway car. Or share the spoils.

I felt sick and weirdly betrayed, like it was me who'd been robbed. Lilou had seemed so nice, so interesting. Was it her job to keep me from noticing what was going on at the other end of the table? Stupid to pretend this was my tragedy, when I was the one who'd introduced them to Harrison. I was guilty by association, had somehow managed to entangle my benevolent host with a ruthless gang of criminal wind instrument masterminds. (*Voleurs d'oboes*. It had a nice ring to it.)

Just at this moment, the bartender called '*Minuit!*'

and everyone moved to pay up and head off. It was illegal, Harrison explained, to be out after 1 a.m. in the heat emergency, so bars closed at midnight to allow for travel.

There was no point rushing to the door to look for Arnaud and Lilou escaping in a taxi, but I did anyway, searching the sparsely peopled street in both directions for oboe thieves as the musicians said their goodbyes. Despite what Lilou had said about people emerging after dark, there wasn't a lot going on. The heat was still intense, thick and inert; everyone who left, left slowly.

I looked one way. And the other. No screeching tyres. Nothing out of the ordinary. Nothing suspicious.

What had I expected?

For a moment I stood gazing into the airless night, drunk, helpless, filled with gloom and regret.

I might have succumbed to self-loathing there and then if a figure on a motorbike hadn't appeared from nowhere, pulled up in front of me and flipped open the visor of the helmet.

'Callum.'

I peered at the half-hidden face. 'Lilou?'

'Need a lift?'

Did I need a lift?

'Put this on,' she said, handing me a spare helmet and indicating the seat behind her. '*On y va.*' Let's go. '*Vite!*'

I teetered for a moment. Was I expected to join the gang? Should I accept the helmet or step back on to the pavement, call Harrison, alert the police, raise the alarm? Was this a kidnapping? Had she taken the fact that my father worked for an oil company to heart and decided to hold me for ransom? It seemed unlikely, but who knew with French women? Who knew with France? Who knew with anything at all?

For an instant I hesitated, and the world seemed to hesitate with me. All summer I'd failed to put myself on the line, to risk speaking French, failed to join in, make friends – and now I faced robbery, abduction, a strange girl, a man whose motives I didn't understand, a purloined oboe – all spread at my feet like the detritus of a car crash.

And then Lilou's eyes caught mine and drew me forward as inexorably as a hand on the front of my shirt, so that I reached out for the helmet and mounted the seat behind her without exercising any particular will of my own.

I was still fumbling to attach the strap under my chin when, with the sound of a 747 speeding down a runway, we flew off into the night.

6

I had been stymied by Élodie's politeness. Unlike Florian, who didn't care if I lived or died, she seemed to feel sorry for me and possibly even a touch sympathetic. Did she like me? Just a little? As a friend? As something ever-so-slightly more? In my anxiety to please, I was happy to accept sympathy in lieu of genuine interest. However, the more she expressed sympathy for my plight (the plight of the social outcast), the less I could speak to her. The less I spoke, the more of an outcast I became. And the more she politely ignored the fact that I was an outcast, the more I loved her.

She must have been aware of her effect on

me. Perhaps she wasn't accustomed to boys falling hopelessly, mutely, in love with her? But that couldn't be. Her line in seduction was honed like a footballer's pass.

At heart I think she was a perfectly decent person. She wanted to be nice. She wanted my summer to be happy. I wanted my summer to be happy too. We were in perfect accord. But the odd friendly comment or sweet smile were all she had to give. Which was fine for her. Crushing for me.

All I wanted was love. And sex, obviously. And for her to think I was funny and smart and desirable, despite the fact that I couldn't speak French and had the seduction skills of a pipefish.

I wanted love so badly, it caused me actual physical pain. It made my head hurt, my guts churn, occupied every waking thought so that I stammered and stumbled and turned bright red whenever she entered a room.

God, it's hell being young.

The Lemoine family was perfect, right down to their symmetry. One father, one mother, one son, one daughter. One dog, one cat. I couldn't help thinking they were just like one of those joke families in my French workbooks. Perfect and unattainable.

While I took over the walking of Titou, Élodie was shadowed everywhere by the cat, a smallish, grey creature called Chichi, who even went into the village with her, riding in the basket of her bicycle or scooting along the lane if she walked. Because of an unfortunate propensity to kill and distribute dismembered mice around the apartment, Chichi wasn't allowed in the bedrooms, which didn't stop her from spending her leisure hours fast asleep on Élodie's pillow, usually with a mangled twitching rodent by her side. Mme Lemoine hated the cat and shooed it away whenever it crossed her path.

Chichi watched me, I suppose because I too crept silently through the house, hiding and dipping around corners so as not to be seen. Maybe she thought I was another cat. Like her, I was fed by the family, my presence tolerated. Élodie occasionally stroked my arm. I could see how Chichi might get the wrong idea about my place in the pecking order.

'*Méchante!*' Élodie would scold her, followed by '*Mon ange, ma louloutte*'. If the mixed messages bothered Chichi, the cat didn't say.

Titou, on the other hand, was a dog. He liked me. He liked walks. He liked chasing rats. He liked life. There was no subtext even with a French dog, which was strangely reassuring. I understood ratters and their agendas, having grown up with Jack Russells – each as cheerful, alert and relentless as the last. Titou spent most of his time flat out in the shade on the tile floor of the flat, panting in the heat, but he rose enthusiastically whenever I came near with the lead, and nothing came between him and pursuit of his sworn enemies.

We set off every morning early, before the temperature rose, turned left up the hill towards the outskirts of the village and then walked straight along the narrow road that led to acres of vineyards bordered by poppy-covered verges. *Coquelicots*. At first, I didn't dare let Titou off the lead for fear he'd see a rat and dart off towards the horizon, leaving me to explain that (along with the rest of my crimes) I'd lost the family dog. But as we got to know each other, he trotted beside me quite companionably – with or without a lead, stopping every metre or so to sniff something fascinating to him, invisible to me. When he did take off, I knew he'd return in his own time, always looking pleased with himself, his muzzle smeared with blood.

It was rare that we came across another soul. The village wasn't on the way to anywhere and there was no reason to travel this road unless you were specifically headed there.

Titou had his best summer ever. I suspected no one in the family had ever paid him this much attention, and certainly he'd never enjoyed so many walks.

From my point of view, he was company, a reason to be out on the roads, walking and thinking. And not being at home where I'd have to talk. Titou replaced the French friend I so dearly hoped to make that summer, and even if he wasn't human, he was still a friend.

Lilou flew over a speed bump, interrupting my reverie with a thud. Why wasn't there a seatbelt on this thing? It seemed a preposterous mode of travel, terrifying and dangerous.

My balance temporarily gone, I swayed perilously until she reached back and steadied my arm, pulling it forward to encircle her waist. It's a miracle I didn't crush her, given how tightly I held on, so frightened that I clamped my eyes shut as we flew around a sharp bend.

Big mistake.

Remember flying up and down on a swing as a child? Remember the joy and the terror of closing your eyes, how dizzy and disorientated you became and the wild swoop in your brain and your stomach? Well, that's what happened to me. With my eyes closed, I instantly lost track of up and down, right and left, and began to spin hopelessly like a top inside my own head.

'*Arrête de bouger!*' Lilou hissed, and I determined to conquer my terror and master the second rule of riding pillion – do not *ever* close your eyes.

'Where are we going?' I shouted.

If she heard she didn't answer, and if she answered, the wind blew her words away.

I tried again. 'Why did Arnaud steal Harrison's oboe?'

No answer. And it appeared that none would be forthcoming either. Which was a shame because I had some very pressing questions. Like: What the hell was her relationship with Arnaud? Had she arrived at the entrance to the bar expressly to carry me off, or was it just a coincidence in timing? And if she'd planned to carry me off – why? Once more my head swirled, this time with fog. But my body remained still.

It was a revelation to me how active riding pillion was. I'd expected it to be a lot like sitting in the back seat of a car, but it required constant rebalancing, like riding a bicycle with no hands. Plus my knees ached. But for some reason I felt safe in Lilou's presence, and with no idea where we were or how I would get back if she dropped me, I decided to trust her. Instead of fighting for balance, I surrendered to fate, relaxed, leaned into the swoop and curl of the road. Kidnapped by destiny.

Well, I said to myself (in perfect, idiomatic Spanish), *que será, será.*

I had no sense of the geography of Paris, other than the general lozenge shape with the river running through it that everyone knows, but that didn't help. A compass might have been useful.

The place we stopped at last was a different Paris, the Paris of gracious nineteenth-century apartment buildings in cream and grey stone with curlicue balconies and gigantic wooden doors. This one had two magnificent olive trees guarding the entrance.

Lilou parked her bike. Removed her helmet. 'Are you OK?' she asked.

I lifted my helmet off a head so hot it felt boiled, and stared at the beautiful buildings, looked up and down the beautiful street at the beautiful shops and restaurants.

'I don't know.' I felt the need to lower my voice. 'I actually have no idea how I am.' And then, 'Why does your bike make such an odd sound?'

'*Électrique*,' she said, like it was obvious.

The almost silent whir. *Électrique. Bien sûr.*

'Zero to one hundred in less than four seconds.'

I felt sick.

'Three hundred and fifty kilometres per hour, six hundred kilometre range.' She grinned like a kid.

Uh-huh. Good to know she could go that fast – preferably with me six hundred kilometres away.

'What's our plan now?' I asked. 'I don't mean to complain, but I'm very hot and very tired.'

She regarded me critically. 'Don't complain then. This is a rare privilege, the best tour of Paris you could ever have.' She took my hand. 'Imagine what you'd pay on Trip Advisor for All-Night Motorbike Paris Mystery Tour with Beautiful Parisian Girl.'

It certainly sounded fun. 'What about the *couvre-feu*?' The curfew.

'Yes,' she said, 'we shall have to be careful. But not yet.'

It was nearly half past twelve.

'Lilou … why did Arnaud steal Harrison's oboe?'

She spun to face me. '*What?*'

'The oboe?' I mimed playing a reeded wind instrument. 'Why did he steal it?'

'What the hell are you talking about?'

Really? 'Um, aren't we looking for a missing oboe? It's worth a lot of money, apparently.'

'Arnaud stole Harrison's oboe? But that's insane. Are you sure? The oboe? Why would he do that?'

How should I know? 'I th-th-thought the two of you were partners in crime. That you conspired with him to steal the oboe.' Not only had I developed a stutter but we both kept saying 'oboe' in a way that suddenly struck me as hilarious and I began to giggle. I was very tired. 'From under the table at the bar.'

Lilou gaped. She looked truly astonished; no one could pretend to be that surprised. 'But why?' she asked. 'Why would he steal Harrison's oboe? He worships Harrison.'

This seemed the least important extenuating circumstance I could think of. Why would anyone steal an oboe in the first place? Worship or no worship.

I shrugged. 'The oboe is gone and no one but Arnaud was near it all evening. Your friend is a secret *voleur d'oboes*.'

'*Hautbois*,' she corrected. 'O-*bwa*.'

Oh yes, I thought. Pronunciation is clearly the main issue here.

'I know nothing about a stolen *hautbois*. All I know is that –' she took a deep breath – 'Arnaud borrowed money from me about a month ago. But the money I lent him wasn't exactly mine. I came to the concert tonight because he promised to pay me back. If I don't get the money back today, I'm in big trouble. He was supposed to bring it with him, but he ran away.' She looked equal parts distressed and angry.

'Why would you lend Arnaud money that wasn't yours?' This seemed the obvious question.

She sighed. 'It's a long story. He said he was desperate.'

Of course he did.

'I made a mistake.' Lilou looked at me. 'So stupid. He convinced me that the loan was only for forty-eight hours, and that he was in danger – grave physical danger.'

'Danger from … whom? Loan sharks? Drug dealers? I guess you didn't get anything in writing. Weren't the circumstances of the loan kind of a red flag?' I said '*drapeau rouge*', not expecting it to translate.

'*Drapeau rouge?*' Lilou looked puzzled. 'It's easy to say you wouldn't have done it. But Arnaud is … He comes from a good family. But he is impetuous and extreme. He has lately become mixed up with some *voyous*, some very heavy types. I am very worried about him. He's not a bad person, really.' She hesitated, looking not entirely convinced by her own speech. 'I wonder about him sometimes.'

'What do you wonder?'

'He's always been attracted to danger, since he was a kid.' She paused, seeking the right words. '*Les histoires compliquées.*' Complications.

I thought about this. 'By complicated, do you mean dodgy?' I didn't know the French equivalent.

'*Douteux?*'

Douteux? We could swap idioms all night.

She shrugged. 'Something is wrong about him. His father had mental health problems but no one in the family talked about it. He was very intelligent, very successful, but also very depressed. *Il s'est suicidé.* I have often wondered if perhaps he was *bipolaire?*'

Bipolar. High and low. Alternately impetuous and depressed. Huh. I'd thought something was off when I met Arnaud. Dog instinct disorder. 'I guess you didn't find out who he needed to pay and how he planned to pay you back so quickly.'

'No.' Lilou sighed and looped the helmet over one arm. She was nearly my height. 'But we're closer than friends, almost blood relatives. How could I refuse to lend money to someone who needed it so badly?'

Despite a history of depression and erratic behaviour? This struck me as dubious in the extreme, justifying poor judgement by citing the moral high ground.

'He hinted that someone was after him. It could have been for any sort of petty crime. Drug money, whatever.'

Pissed-off thugs with crowbars. 'Maybe he stole the oboe to sell and plans to pay you back that way.'

She frowned. 'That would be the most idiotic way of raising money ever conceived. And he's not going to be able to sell it tonight, is he? Except maybe to some twenty-four-hour pawnshop. Which will give him next to nothing for it. Even Arnaud's not that much of a fool.' She said '*un fou*'. I had no trouble with the word 'crazy'.

'Then why do you think he took it?'

She was silent for a moment, shook her head. 'He has some sort of plan; said he would tell me about it when we met, after the concert. And then the minute I got up from the table, he ran away.'

'And what, if you don't mind my asking, am I doing here?' I barely dared ask in case she suddenly remembered that there was no point to me and dumped me like last week's baguette.

Instead she sighed. 'How could I leave you behind?'

Quite easily I'd have thought, and also, that is not an answer. And also again, what exactly did that mean? Did Lilou find me so irresistible that she genuinely wanted to extend our time together? Or was I some sort of hostage? I forced my brain to be ruthlessly logical and voted against irresistible. Which left hostage.

Really? I was much too tired to think.

7

Lilou marched up to the gigantic door and rang the bell. Once, twice.

Someone answered at last. What sounded like a pack of wolves howled down the intercom and a voice said, '*Oui? C'est qui?*'

'*C'est Lilou, Jeannine, desolée pour l'heure!*' Lilou apologised for ringing after midnight and said she was looking for Arnaud, was hoping perhaps Jeannine might have some idea where to find him?

There was a silence at the other end of the intercom. And then the woman said simply, '*Alors, oui,*' and buzzed us in through the little door set into the huge door.

The lift, for which I was grateful, was the old-fashioned sort with ornate metalwork and a retractable door. Lilou pulled it shut and pressed the green enamelled number 5, where a woman of about fifty in a yellow and pink silk kimono stood in the doorway.

She ordered the two large dogs to lie down, and when I saw her in profile, the resemblance to Arnaud was striking. They both had aristocratic features – arched eyebrows, a long, fine nose, high cheekbones. The greyhounds could have been distant relatives.

If this was Arnaud's mother, and Arnaud was Lilou's stepbrother, then Arnaud's mother's husband must be Lilou's father. Had I got that right? I went over it again in my head but couldn't untangle it.

'Come in, my dear,' Jeannine said, kissing Lilou warmly, then turned to me with a little frown and a slight tilt of the head. *And you are?*

Lilou said, 'Jeannine, I'd like you to meet Callum, my English friend. Callum, this is Arnaud's mother. Madame Toussaint.'

In perfect English, Mme Toussaint said, 'I am very pleased to make your acquaintance. Though perhaps not under these circumstances.'

I smiled wanly and nodded, unclear as to the precise nature of the circumstances.

While they talked, I looked around the room. I'd never seen an apartment big enough for a gigantic marble fireplace and a grand piano. Was it coincidence that the huge grey sofas perfectly matched the dogs? I wondered which came first, whether Mme Toussaint had sent swatches off to a puppy farm. Mirrored tables held Chinese lamps and stacks of fat books on modern art; an abstract painting filled the entire back wall with brilliant streaks of colour. On the long wall that overlooked the street, three sets of doors opened on to narrow balconies – still closed and shuttered to keep out the heat.

'I'm in so much trouble,' Lilou was saying. 'I lent Arnaud money. I need it back now and he's disappeared.'

'O! *Je suis tellement desolée.*' The woman shook her head with an unhappy chirp. 'My son can be so difficult, and you have always been good to him. However, my dear Lilou, had I been present, I might have suggested you not lend him money.'

Hindsight is a wonderful thing.

Jeannine began to interrogate Lilou, with a combination of anxiety and weariness, as if this were familiar territory. I realised only gradually that nearly everything the older woman said in French was crystal clear to me. It was a revelation, like wearing glasses for the first time and I wondered if it was her precise, old-fashioned diction. Or perhaps the immersion method of learning French had finally worked – half a bottle of wine and the same subject discussed over and over.

'He was here,' she said. 'A few days ago. Because

he missed me, he claimed. I knew something wasn't right, but I was happy to see him and didn't want to question his motives. And then this.'

My attention had softened somewhat, but when the woman pointed to an empty space on the wall above the piano, I snapped to attention. A bare rectangle stood out bright against the faded wallpaper – the outline of a missing painting.

'*Le Matisse*,' she said to Lilou.

'*Le Matisse?*' Lilou's jaw dropped.

I looked from one to the other. Had I heard right? Did they mean Matisse, the great modern artist generally found only in large national museums? Impossible. He'd obviously had a much less famous son, Gerard Matisse. Or not to be sexist, a daughter. Monica Matisse. But a large thick book on the table below, with the name *Henri Matisse* printed on the spine, offered a clue.

'It belonged to my father,' Mme Toussaint explained, 'a great patron of the arts. Someday it would have belonged to Arnaud if he'd had a bit of patience. But to steal it?' She shook her head.

Lilou gaped. 'You have told the police?'

The woman shook her head vehemently; no, of course she had not told the police. 'He is my son,' she said. And then by way of explanation, or an attempt at one, 'And he means well.'

Could we all agree on that? Possibly not.

I was confused. A priceless family painting, stolen by Arnaud. But why? 'Why?' seemed to be the most popular question raised by Arnaud's activities.

Mme Toussaint took us through to the kitchen and put the kettle on for tea.

'He says he has a plan,' Lilou told Jeannine. 'He told me yesterday. But I don't know what that plan is. He ran away before I could ask him. With a valuable oboe. Also stolen.'

'*Un hautbois?*' The older woman looked confused.

'*Un hautbois.*'

'*Pourquoi un hautbois?*'

Well, yes, I thought, that's the million-dollar question. 'We *think* he took it,' I said. To be fair, we didn't know for sure, even though all the circumstantial evidence shouted his name.

Mme Toussaint glanced at me briefly. 'Perhaps to sell?' She put tea bags and hot water into bone china cups and handed one to me. 'It is all most unfortunate,' she said, with what appeared to be deep sadness.

The tea smelled of hibiscus and tasted of nothing.

They began talking about Arnaud's '*situation*'; he had *des problèmes psychologiques*, Mme Toussaint said, and was therefore not responsible for his own behaviour.

I could see that this line did not convince Lilou. Mme Toussaint never mentioned what exactly *les problèmes* might be, nor was there any suggestion that it might be something more than ordinary neurosis. But Lilou had said that Arnaud's father killed himself. Surely that might suggest a history of something other than social anxiety.

Slowly, through a brain thick as treacle, I considered more clues. Arnaud's mother owned a beautiful apartment in an expensive neighbourhood, not to mention a genuine Matisse – well, not any more – so Arnaud was rich. I supposed that's what Lilou had meant by 'a good family'. So why was he stealing things? Valuable things. Did he need money for drugs? Were the Matisse and the *hautbois* somehow connected? Arnaud's rampage had the feeling of a mad treasure hunt. One post-Impressionist French painting, one woodwind instrument …

'I am certain,' Mme Toussaint said, 'that these are simply the actions of a misguided young man.' But she looked distressed.

I'd look distressed too if someone had stolen a priceless painting from me, particularly if it had been my son, so I couldn't shop him to the police.

Mme Toussaint clapped her hands, pushed back

her chair and stood. 'But now you must go. It is almost one! *Vite, vite! Le couvre-feu!*'

Lilou stood too. 'Please forgive the intrusion,' she said in formal French. 'We will keep you up to date.'

'I simply want him to be safe.' His mother's face was blotchy with emotion. 'And you too. Now go!'

I suspected she didn't know about the drug dealers (were there drug dealers?) and the rest. But despite insisting Arnaud was merely misguided, she may have had her suspicions.

Mme Toussaint kissed Lilou, shook my hand, opened the front door for us and watched as we descended the staircase. Lilou at speed, me dragging behind like a tired child.

'But what about the *couvre-feu*?' I whined like a tired child too.

'We will be careful.' By 'careful' she obviously didn't mean carefully going home to bed, which was the only truly careful thing to do.

Perhaps I could ask Lilou to drop me at

Harrison's? He'd surely be worried. And even if he wasn't, I was. I really didn't want to be shot by a roving SWAT team, or whatever its equivalent was in France, and I was certain Lilou's plans involved remaining out after curfew.

'The painting,' she murmured. 'It makes everything more serious. Do you have any idea what a painting like that is worth?'

The question may have been rhetorical, but I had a general idea. The currency didn't matter. Pounds, euros, drachmas. It had to be worth a fortune.

'What is he up to? Why on earth would he steal what's practically his own property? He can't be thinking of selling it.' She paused. And then, responding to her own question, murmured, 'I don't know why. I have no idea why.'

I added it to my long list of unfathomables.

8

We left the glamorous sixteenth arrondissement with its honey-coloured buildings, ornate balconies and broad avenues. On the way, we drove around the Arc de Triomphe, so recognisable I didn't even need Lilou to tap my thigh and point, like I might have missed Paris's greatest – second-greatest – monument, lit up golden against the night sky.

The city's largest roundabout should have been jammed with cars, even at this time of night, but the streets were eerily empty, thanks to the curfew.

Through the silent night we rode, handsome restaurants and expensive hotels giving way to empty shopfronts as the city gradually morphed into something poorer, grittier, less familiar. Figures in pairs and small groups slid in and out of the shadows. In this part of Paris, curfew enforcement didn't appear to have the same urgency.

Occasionally we passed an ambulance or police car, usually headed towards tents marked *SAUVETAGE* which appeared at regular intervals along main roads. Lilou explained that they provided first aid for the very old or very young, the ill, or anyone medically affected by the heat. To be safe we avoided everyone, drove slowly down deserted side roads and alleyways, always keeping a look-out for bored cops. I turned my head away, like an ostrich not wanting to look. If I couldn't see them, maybe they couldn't see us.

Paris changed constantly as we rode. Window displays, number of potholes, posters, bus shelter ads. Some blocks featured burned-out cars and smouldering heaps of rubbish. After a while, graffitied sixties buildings became sprawling concrete council estates that had probably been visionary when first built. Groups of kids in shorts and cut-off T-shirts hung out on the streets talking and smoking. The *couvre-feu* barely seemed to exist in these neighbourhoods, along with the rule of law. We were waved at, applauded for our defiance as we passed. In some places the smell of weed was so strong it coloured the air.

Lilou risked a long straight road, where the reassuring hum of the bike and fatigue got the better of me and I momentarily dozed off. Feeling me list dramatically to one side, Lilou grabbed my arm and hissed, '*Attention!*'

Well, I thought, thoroughly awake now, slumping off a motorbike at speed is one way to sort out your future.

Lilou was not so sanguine. She pulled over to the side of the road and turned on me, furious. '*Tu dois rester éveillé! Tu comprends?*'

I nodded meekly. Stay awake. I got it. But really, I wanted to tell her I wasn't the sort of person who did well without sleep, and perhaps she should have made further enquiries before choosing a partner for her all-night adventure.

Anticipating the impression this would make, I kept my mouth shut.

She started the bike again and we powered on through the steamy night, the quiet whir of the motorbike carving a path through the hot air. At last she braked, and swerved down the side of a tower block, cut the engine, and turned sharp left down a ramp into an underground area full of huge recycling bins. She'd been here before.

Lilou pulled off her helmet and shook out her damp hair. 'Arnaud stays here sometimes. Come on. If he's here, we'll surprise him.'

Looking for Arnaud would have made a good name for our all-night drama, where we chase a criminal (of good family) all over Paris, hoping to recover a variety of valuable but unrelated objects and a stack of money that was probably long gone.

It was hard to know whether this whole situation was impossibly mysterious or whether I had merely failed to comprehend some simple fact at the centre of it all that would have clarified everything. The problem of speaking the language like a ten-year-old was the near-infinite opportunity for misunderstanding.

'Callum!' Lilou had started up the stairs, taking them at a run. I plodded slowly behind, hauling myself along step by step, wondering if it would be acceptable to wait at ground level so as not to exert myself needlessly. It was too hot. Too hot for this. Too hot for anything. I might have waited at the bottom except that, knowing Lilou, she'd get to the top, dive out a window, get caught up by a passing eagle and disappear forever.

So I climbed.

She reached the top floor and pounded on the door. 'Saïd? Arnaud? *Ouvrez!*'

A very dozy-looking guy in boxers and T-shirt opened the door, rubbing his eyes. It was not Arnaud.

'Lilou? Quelle heure est-il?'

It was 2 a.m. Saïd opened the door to his apartment and let us in, all the while staring at Lilou in bewilderment.

The place was such a mess I couldn't take it in all at once. Posters and leaflets teetered in stacks everywhere. I could read *CLIMAT* on some of them so I figured he was part of some climate protest team. Sport was obviously his second passion, with posters of Paris Saint-Germain players neatly pinned to the wall, the only orderly elements in a room chaotic with books, IT equipment, protest detritus and clothes piled up on the floor. I tried not to step on his stuff, but it was impossible. There was no clear space to walk.

Lilou spoke to Saïd in a rapid undertone. He looked somewhat dazed (as I imagined you might if rudely woken in the middle of your best REM sleep), ran his hands through his hair, sat down, stood up again, rubbed his eyes, paced about.

I guessed Arnaud was not hiding under Saïd's bed.

Bits and pieces of the conversation made sense to me, him saying no, he hadn't seen Arnaud, yes, he agreed that Arnaud had been behaving strangely and was probably up to something, no, he didn't know what, and by the way, no, he didn't care all that much, and why was Lilou waking him up in the middle of the night? Arnaud was *her* brother – stepbrother, *désolé* – and not really his problem.

The more confusing conversation was the one about the money that Arnaud owed Lilou.

I understood that the loan was connected to Lilou's job, but not exactly what that connection was. This was a genuine failure of understanding on my part; I'm sure I'd missed out something that might have explained it.

Saïd obviously liked Lilou, and wanted to help, but possibly did not like Arnaud, and thus didn't care so much about helping. The tie-breaker was

2 a.m. Which I understood. No one much feels like helping anyone at that hour.

As for me, I found that my brain could translate the hell out of a conversation at first, but as the minutes ticked by, I began to lose ground. Words crashed into each other, transformed into similar-sounding phrases and ended up piled all over the place in messy heaps like Saïd's dirty clothes. Ten minutes into an exchange, they could have been speaking Elvish for all I could understand.

Saïd listened to Lilou's story, one I'd heard a number of times now. He opened his mouth to speak, then closed it. I guessed he was about to ask the popular question about why she had lent Arnaud a large amount of money that wasn't hers in the first place – whose was it? – and then thought better of it due to some instinct. Lilou did not look like a woman who failed to appreciate her own error of judgement.

Eventually Saïd took out his phone and said

something that made her kiss him on both cheeks and sweep out the door with me trailing behind.

'What was all that?' I asked.

She galloped down the stairs ahead of me. 'He's not there.'

You don't say.

'But Saïd had a suggestion. He's texted Arnaud's ex-girlfriend. They were together a long time and she saw him recently. She might know where he is.'

'Why doesn't Arnaud have an address, like normal people?'

She sighed. 'Arnaud lives here, he lives there. He deals in drugs, information, all sorts of stolen stuff …'

'Priceless paintings. And oboes. And remind me? He plays classical music.'

She stopped and turned to face me. 'Why shouldn't a musician also be a criminal drug user?'

No reason, Lilou. It's obviously the latest form of intersectionality. Violinist, drug addict, cat burglar.

'He does good things too. He's a disrupter.'

That's all right then. 'They're the ones who glue themselves to roads and paintings?' To myself I thought: And in this particular case, disrupt the lives of everyone around them with their annoying behaviour.

'*Oui*. I admire him.'

Permit me to abstain. 'You don't think he's going to glue himself to the Matisse?'

Lilou dismissed this with a contemptuous wave of her arm, but it bothered me. Might there be a connection between disruption and the things he was stealing? Something about the painting worried me. Van Gogh, Klimt, Leonardo, Botticelli, Vermeer … they'd all been the subject of climate protest events. Why not Matisse? Particularly as Arnaud conveniently had one on his person. And it practically belonged to him anyway.

I'd never thought terribly hard about the people who vandalised priceless works of art. But I guessed

Lilou must be right, it was admirable. The world burned, and people like me dutifully studied for exams. I knew it wasn't good enough.

'He sounds like quite a multitasker,' I muttered in English.

But Lilou understood, and my sarcasm did not impress her. 'He is passionate. Not so enamoured of reason. He wants solutions. His plans are not always, shall we say, prudent, but his purpose is pure.'

Uh-huh. His aim may have been true, but to me he sounded like a loose cannon. Disguised as a red herring. Hurtling brakeless down a mountain.

'There's a big climate demo this afternoon,' Lilou told me. 'Everyone's pushing for the new oil tax to be approved. Our future teeters on a knife's edge. The future of the world too.'

The future of the world? Was that all? At this moment I was ashamed to say my primary concern was my own future, when any moment I might be shot for being a foreign national out at night when it was entirely illegal to be out at night. Call me selfish.

And then we were back on the bike, my arms around Lilou's waist, the engine of the bike sounding its soft whine as she gunned it through the Paris night once more.

9

My infatuation for Élodie made me sick, literally weak and feverish. I fantasised about her, about us, about returning to the house with Titou and finding her waking from a nap, of her taking me by the hand, leading me to her bedroom and saying, 'I have dreamed about this, *mon cher*.'

I had never had sex with another person but imagined that Élodie would be patient and tender, amused by my inexperience rather than disgusted by it. And in the tradition of older women seducing young virgins, I would exceed all her expectations. My naivety, my enthusiasm, my gratitude would win the day.

Within this protracted fantasy I became a sex

zombie, a silent embodiment of longing. It occurred to me that I probably seemed creepy to her. Cloying and stalkerish.

I can't think about it.

Lilou and I were nearly two hours past curfew when she tapped my leg and pointed to a police car some way up ahead. In seconds there were two uniformed men standing in the road waving a search-light at us, blinding, full in our eyes.

I knew very little about the *Police Nationale*, having no prior cause to annoy them. They were smartly dressed, all in black, with vicious looking weapons. I hoped they weren't trigger-happy.

Lilou took hold of my hand and pulled it tight around her waist, and I braced myself for whatever lunatic plan ensued. I prayed she'd decide to surrender quietly and receive a polite reprimand before being sent home to sleep.

Pause here for hollow existential laughter.

Lilou pushed the accelerator to the floor, then

spun the bike, skidding sideways into a U-turn, my knee a blade's width from the road. Then it was zero to flat-out, and together we split the air like an arrow. My lungs collapsed and my heart lay on the road six seconds behind my body as I clutched Lilou for dear life, wishing I wasn't here on this road in Paris on this lethal bike with this lethal girl, unable to breathe, adrenalin replacing blood, fear in every cell of my body, nothing in my head but terror and the certainty I'd soon be dead.

I turned back to look and, just for the record, there were two cars racing up behind us, sirens blaring.

Also for the record, turn your head and your body follows, which is not a good look on a speeding bike. Unbalanced, we wobbled, and for a few grim seconds Lilou fought to control the shrieking tyres as they slipped sideways out of true, a shudder convulsing up through her, then through me, while I thought, *Oh God, we're going to crash and burn and die*, and panic snatched at me, gripping my throat while Lilou wrestled gravity and acceleration and I begged those forces not to kill us both. *Be still, be still, be still.* I made myself inert as clay and light as ash and at last felt gravity release its death grip and we balanced and steadied and were once more eating up ground. Lilou controlled the beast, but took time out to elbow me, hard.

Blinded by sweat and terrified tears, I welcomed the pain.

The police car behind us was fast but Lilou was master of the universe. Me? Still petrified, mouth full of dust, my sphincter too clenched even to shit myself with fear. But I'd learned my lesson. She banked hard into a narrow road, made a sharp reverse turn, and this time I followed her and the bike, adjusted, thinking: *I am the wheels, the driver, eyes trained on the road ahead, flowing, flying.* Through short irregular passageways we serpentined and shimmied like a sidewinder snake. Oh well, I thought, at least if we die I might get some rest.

Darting and dodging, travelling fast, on side streets now, I could hear sirens behind us but they weren't coming closer. I prayed to God no stray child or cat or fox stepped out in front of the bike, setting off dominoes of extinction. *Don't look, don't turn away, don't close your eyes.* Despite the exhilaration of speed, I felt sick with terror.

Loved it too.

We were lost in a maze of lefts and rights and switchbacks. No one knew Paris this well, not even Lilou. I was sure she was as lost as I was. And then she spied an open garage and pulled up over a kerb, drove into it and hauled the door shut behind us before cutting the engine.

It should be silent in here, I thought, but it wasn't, my rasping breath so loud and ragged I felt sure it would alert every cop for miles.

For a second, I held my breath and heard nothing. No sirens, no shouting, no pursuit. And then the panting again, harsh, fearful breathing I couldn't control. It had probably been going on for hours, masked by the sound of the bike. I fell back on the top-box, arms weak and useless as a baby's. I was shaking uncontrollably and when I tried to climb off, my legs collapsed.

'Take your time,' she said. 'We'll rest here a bit.'

I'm glad she didn't expect me to start sprinting.

Ladders and wooden trellises hung from big metal hooks all around us, lining the walls, along with shelves of nails, drill bits and screwdrivers, all carefully organised by size. Lilou's motorbike slotted in nicely next to the lawnmower.

After about ten minutes, my breathing quiet, my pulse slowed, Lilou suggested we go. 'We'll avoid that road,' she told me, like it wasn't obvious.

'What if they're waiting for us?' Somewhere in the distance I could hear a church strike 3 a.m.

'It's a curfew offence. They're just bored. It's not like we robbed a bank, I doubt they'll shoot us.' *Cambriolé une banque.* I'd never heard the expression before. 'Let me see if you're ready,' she said, holding out her own arm by way of example, palm down, steady as steel. I did the same and my limbs no longer shook.

'Good.' She nodded, opening the door of the garage, checking the street right and left. All silent; the city asleep, noise stifled in the blanket of heat.

10

My life had officially taken a turn for the Twilight Zone.

Luckily, I didn't have time to think about what I was doing and why, what with holding on for dear life the whole time. I wasn't ready to die, in part because I needed to know how this crazy story would end.

The bike ticked stealthily across Paris. Through half-shut eyes I clocked each neighbourhood – this one expensive and tidy, this exuberant and colourful with music blaring out of windows and rubbish piled up at every door. It turned out that Paris was not, as I'd imagined, a single perfect beauty, but a fascinating commotion of different moods and personalities, races, religions, cuisines, music and manners of dress. I liked it better for its unruly chaos, its varied whims, all united by a single language spoken with a thousand different accents. Including mine.

Lilou stopped suddenly in front of a tiny Algerian café next to a bright blue shopfront. The café was buzzing with customers at nearly 4 a.m. and you might easily have missed the blank frontage of the address next door. Distracted, I forgot to brace, and cracked the back of her helmet with mine. She turned around and rolled her eyes but said nothing.

We dismounted. I followed her lead, approaching the empty shopfront in silence.

Lilou rang the bell, and a well-built bouncer in a dark suit opened the door and politely asked what he could do for us.

'I'd like to see Meriam,' she said. 'I know she's busy, but I just need a minute, *s'il vous plaît*. I'm Lilou, she's expecting me.'

The bouncer looked us up and down, then stepped aside and directed us into what felt like a Tardis, through the shabby blue door into an unexpectedly large chandeliered lobby. He guided us to a side room, moodily lit and entirely furnished in pink and red velvet – chairs, sofas, even pink velvet wallpaper. I had the feeling that if you turned the lights full on, the place would look like a grubby version of Barbie's Dreamhouse, but low golden lighting made it glow. The hum of the air conditioning was almost drowned out by piped-in music, someone with a husky voice singing in German.

'Where are we?' I whispered. 'What is this place?'

Lilou shushed me, the bouncer left, and we waited in silence. She didn't meet my eyes.

He returned a few minutes later to tell Lilou that Meriam was on her way. And then one of the most beautiful women I'd ever seen opened the door and strode to embrace Lilou with a little cry of welcome.

'Lilou!' Meriam moved gracefully, entirely at ease despite wearing nothing but a flimsy pale green set of silk lingerie and matching (very) high heels.

She and Lilou kissed. 'Oh, *ma chère*, I am so happy to see you!'

Meriam turned to me. 'Hello,' she said, 'I am Meriam.' And extended her hand.

I took it, too nonplussed to speak.

There was nothing coy about her, or about Lilou in her presence. I tried to follow their example and behave as if all this were entirely ordinary (whatever 'this' was), but I felt certain my unease shone like a beacon.

'This is your first sex club?' Meriam asked. 'It's not so different from any other club. I serve in the bar, sometimes I dance, and I try to keep clients from fighting. The only difference is that people come here to have sex.' She looked at me sternly. 'Though not with me.'

I nodded. Crystal clear.

'Lilou,' she said, taking in the leather jacket and helmet. 'You came on the bike? In this heat? You must be half dead.'

Lilou smiled. 'I should try wearing less.'

'You would look very nice in less. But you haven't come at this hour for a chat? Tell me why you are here.' She sat down beside Lilou on the sofa.

'It's Arnaud,' she said.

Meriam snorted. 'Yes, of course it's Arnaud. I should have known. It's always Arnaud. What has he done this time?'

'Stolen some things, an oboe, a painting, money … It's valuable things he's taken, and he keeps hinting about some plan he has.'

I could tell Meriam was unimpressed. 'I saw him last week and he seemed about the same as usual. Full of crazy plans. When he's like that …' Meriam shrugged. 'He came asking for his job back, but management laughed in his face. He caused enough trouble last time and there's still a question of missing money. You know he was running side actions in the club, selling services we would never offer, like underage girls, drugs and worse, then taking a percentage. There are limits, Lilou, he has no shame.'

'I know.' Lilou fidgeted. I knew she felt responsible.

My picture of Arnaud was filling out nicely. An aristocratic violin-playing climate activist, thief and pimp. This wasn't the sort of person I'd had much exposure to previously.

'He took the rejection calmly, had a drink and then asked if *I* would take him back.' Meriam shook her head. 'Listen, I know he's your stepbrother, but I've truly had enough of that guy. There isn't a straight bone in his body. Everything he did when we were together was crooked. He called himself a climate warrior but was that why he needed money? Or was it the drugs?'

And addict.

Lilou looked distressed. She tried to interrupt, but Meriam ploughed on.

108

'I know about his father and I know what you think. You will tell me he's not well. But does corruption run in the family too? Is that a medical condition or does it just give him an excuse to behave badly? Is there a gene that turns you into a pimp?' Meriam stood and paced the pink room. The amazing glow it gave her skin made me understand the point of pink walls. 'He could be lovely, I know that. I was fond of him; would I have gone out with him otherwise? But there's a screw loose. Too many drugs, too much hustle. I don't think he was so bad when I first met him. Or maybe he was, and I just didn't notice.'

'What did he say when you told him no?'

'He took it reasonably well,' Meriam said. 'We talked for a few minutes, but not about any plans he had. And then he left. No forwarding address.'

Lilou paused. 'I wouldn't expect you to take him back. But I don't know what to do.'

'Why do you have to do anything? Why are you involved all of a sudden?'

Lilou didn't answer.

Meriam frowned. 'Don't tell me it's your money he stole? You lent him money? I don't believe it. You did! Well, you'll never see it again. And if he owes you money, you won't see him again in a hurry either.'

I wasn't catching the whole narrative, but my brain translated the highlights.

Lilou's head dropped back on the sofa. Of course, she'd been up all night too.

'No wonder he's missing,' Meriam said. 'He is totally *pas fiable*.'

I looked at Lilou. '*Pas fiable*,' she said. 'Unreliable.'

Meriam had her legs crossed and one arm dangling off the edge of her chair. She was prepos-terously lovely and I had to stop myself staring. 'I think we need coffee,' she said, and went to the door to call for the bouncer, who bounced up again. 'Coffee, please, Rémy. For three if you don't mind?'

Rémy's presence was large and frightening but he seemed happy enough to fetch coffee for beautiful Meriam. He arrived back with a brass Arabic coffee pot, three small cups and some honey cake on a tray.

'Thank you, *chéri*,' she said, pouring out the coffee and passing one to me and one to Lilou. 'The cake is from the café next door.'

I hadn't realised I was starving until that moment. After watching me wolf down one piece, Meriam passed me hers. I tried refusing but she waved me away.

The cake tasted of rose water and cardamom; the coffee was thick and black. Sugar and caffeine; the combination brought me a few steps closer to human.

'Forget about the money,' Meriam was saying to Lilou. 'There's nothing at all you can do. And the painting more or less belongs to him anyway, doesn't it? You could go completely crazy trying to get Arnaud to pay back what he owes. He owes money to every shady dealer in Paris. And keeping track of his crazy schemes …' She paused. 'Impossible. But *un hautbois*? That is strange. *Pourquoi un hautbois?*'

I had started to wonder if this was the most commonly uttered phrase in the French language.

Lilou sighed. 'Never mind the *hautbois*. I'll lose my job if I don't get the money back by tomorrow morning,' she said. 'If I lose my job, I can't pay my rent and will also lose my apartment. And my bike. There will be nothing left to my life.'

'If I had the money, I would give it to you,' said Meriam, kissing her friend's hand. 'But it's only money. There is always another job and another flat, and even,' she said, 'another motorbike.' She lit a cigarette. 'And another man, if one were foolish enough to want one.' Meriam looked at me and her eyes flickered wickedly. 'I beg your pardon, Callum.'

Unwilling representative of all the world's men, I nodded forgiveness.

Lilou looked grim. 'I don't want to go to jail.'

Jail?

'Why would you go to jail?'

'It's complicated. The money wasn't exactly mine to lend.'

I saw Meriam's eyes flare and then she abruptly changed the subject. 'At least they're predicting perfect weather for the demo.' She most definitely didn't want to delve any deeper into Lilou's predicament. 'Hot as hell. Another reminder that the world is burning.'

They continued to talk about the afternoon demo, and the vote that was taking place in the French parliament, and the fossil fuel tax. The turnout was expected to be huge. Lilou's lobbying group had been promoting it for weeks.

I ran over all the facts and questions in my head.

Lilou lent Arnaud money (for what?) because he said he was in danger (what danger?). She had trusted him to return it quickly so she could repay … whom?

A month had passed.

He had come to the bar last night to pay her back; at least, that's what she expected.

The money hadn't materialised.

Arnaud had disappeared. With Harrison's oboe, the second purloined object, the first being a valuable painting that belonged to future-him.

And now Lilou was going to lose her job, her home and her motorbike. And possibly go to jail. Because the money she'd lent Arnaud wasn't hers. Why would she lose her job? Had she 'borrowed' it from someone important? Or perhaps, I thought suddenly, from work?

I was missing a few links. But did I really care? The details weren't any of my business and these people barely more than strangers. I glanced at Lilou, her sad expression and lovely eyes, and felt a dull pain in my chest.

Meriam had written an address on a piece of paper (there were no pockets in her outfit for a phone) and handed it to Lilou. 'Try this place,' she said. 'It belongs to a guy we both knew who works in Brussels. You never know. Arnaud must be running out of places to hide.'

Lilou took the paper and motioned to pay for the coffee, but Meriam waved her away, kissed her three times and wished her '*bonne chance*'. Adding as an afterthought, 'And be careful of Arnaud, please. He may be your relative, but he is always trouble.'

Then she was off, dissolving back into the club like sugar in rum, waving to me as an afterthought.

'OK, let's go,' Lilou said.

I'd given up asking where. Lilou bid Rémy farewell and we passed a smartly dressed, grey-haired older couple coming in as we left. I tried not to imagine them … at all.

And then we were outside, staring at the bland exterior of a building that hid a treasure trove of secrets. My education continued.

'One more try,' said Lilou. 'Montreuil.'

'What's Montreuil?' I fiddled with my helmet strap once more, fatigue making me clumsy.

'A neighbourhood,' she said. 'East, across the *périphérique*.'

Whatever that was.

The accelerating whir of the engine drowned out any further explanation. As we flew off at speed, I managed not to smash my head against Lilou's helmet.

Well done, Callum. I congratulated myself, knowing no one else would.

11

We crossed over the ring road and entered yet another Paris. It was just beginning to get light.

African and Arab shopkeepers set up stalls, dragging boxes of exotic fruit and veg out on to the street to the accompaniment of overlapping dance music from competing speakers. Even at this hour, double- and triple-parked delivery vans slowed travel, and I struggled to sit motionless behind Lilou in the stop-and-start traffic.

Eventually we came to a squarish 1960s apartment block. 'Come on,' Lilou said, kicking down the stand and climbing off the bike. I followed slowly. Not only was I tired, but every part of my body ached: back, neck, legs and arms. Buttocks. Shoulders. Wrists. Even my feet hurt. It took a few minutes before I could stand fully upright.

Lilou rang the bell. There was no answer. She rang again, and eventually just leaned on the buzzer until a crackly male voice shouted, 'Get the fuck off my bell before I come down and kill you,' or some near equivalent in French. It was not yet 5 a.m. Whoever it was had a point.

She begged to be let in, but the connection was no longer live. The occupant had disappeared.

'What do we do now?'

'We wait.'

I thought about this. 'Couldn't we just go home?'

'No,' she said, but at once seemed to regret her tone, and when she looked at me her face softened. 'I'm sorry, Callum. You didn't ask to be mixed up in this.'

Truer words had never been spoken. I shrugged. Shrugging hurt.

She put her hands on my shoulders (which hurt). 'If we could just find Arnaud, we could end this whole chase, go home and forget the whole night ever happened.'

Tired as I was, I wasn't sure I wanted to forget that this whole night had ever happened. Nor was I likely to. I'd never had a more exciting, exhausting, perplexing night in my life. And it wasn't over yet.

But more to the point, I felt unconvinced that finding Arnaud would do Lilou any good at all. It seemed unlikely that her money would make an appearance even if she did find him. Surely, if he'd intended to pay her back, he'd have done so at the bar. In which case, what was the point of chasing him around Paris all night?

I could have said all this, but my language skills were flagging, and Lilou looked too despondent for logic. Instead, I asked, 'How much money does Arnaud owe you?'

She sighed. 'Two thousand euros.'

119

'Where did the money come from, Lilou?'

The question at last.

She hesitated. 'I borrowed it from my departmental budget at work.'

'Borrowed?' I was shocked. 'In England we call that embezzling.'

Lilou nodded. 'In France too. But only if I don't return it in time. So far, no one has noticed. The monthly audit happens first thing tomorrow morning.' She shook her head. 'It was such a mistake. I only wanted to help.'

'Excuse me for expressing an opinion after so little acquaintance with you both, but Arnaud seems to need more help than you or anyone else could give in a lifetime.'

She said nothing.

Right. 'Can't you borrow it from someone else?'

'Two thousand euros? How many people do you know who could lend you that sort of money?'

I blinked. 'I will.'

'Don't be stupid,' she snorted. 'You can't even pay for coffee.'

This was true. But I did have a credit card, loaded with money for emergencies. And here I was, nearly eighteen hours into a bona fide emergency, and I still hadn't touched it.

The idea of handing that sort of sum over to Lilou was absurd, but then, everything about the past eighteen hours had been absurd, from skipping out on the train to sitting on a pavement in an outer suburb of Paris surrounded by halal meat while the sun rose. I wished I could go back to Lilou's flat, to anyone's flat really, for an hour or two of sleep. That would be worth almost any amount of money right now. If I gave her the money, would she stop chasing Arnaud? Could we go home to bed – or at least to sleep?

'Here,' I said, holding out my phone. 'Give me your bank details and I'll transfer it over. It's yours. I know you're good for it.' I didn't know any such thing, I only said that to flatter her, because frankly, I had no way to pay back two thousand euros and my father would kill me if I told him I'd given it all to some girl I barely knew.

Some girl.

My judgement was skewed, I was too tired to think, and I already had kind of a bad track record of falling in love with French women more or less at random. But there was no denying that Lilou was some girl. Some woman.

She took hold of my hands and looked at me solemnly. 'You would do that?'

I nodded.

'And trust me to pay you back?'

I shrugged. 'If you don't, like Meriam said, it's only money. I'll get a job in September and work to reimburse my dad. He'll be OK with that.'

This was a colossal lie. He would not be OK with it. It would confirm to him every negative thing he'd ever accused me of being – profligate, gullible, impractical, reckless. But for the moment, I didn't care what anyone else thought.

Lilou was staring at me. 'I don't believe you.'

'What don't you believe? That my dad wouldn't mind? That I'll get a job? That I'll lend you the money?'

'All of it.'

'Look,' I said. 'I don't know why you took me along with you tonight, but it's been amazing and weird and it's made me rethink pretty much everything I thought I knew.'

It *had* caused me to think. About how one person (in this case Arnaud) could be so chaotic and fucked up that his entire life and the lives of all the people around him were dragged into a whirlpool of crisis. About one horrible summer and how it wasn't, in fact, the end of the world. About France, and how being self-conscious and afraid to fail meant I hadn't given it a chance. About heat. About climate. About responsibility. About risk.

About Lilou.

I didn't say any of this out loud. It was enough to say it inside my head.

'As for the money –' I looked at her – 'my parents expect me to screw up anyway. They sent me away this summer to try to jump-start my personality.' I said 'jump-start' in English because I had no idea how to say it in French.

Lilou looked blank.

'*Activer? Actionner?*' I was just guessing, but she nodded.

'How old are you, Callum?'

I thought of adding a couple of years but realised it wouldn't help. '*Dix-sept.*'

She shook her head. 'Do you realise how ridiculous that is? What your parents expect of you? To be organised at seventeen? Who would want that? No one interesting is sensible before forty. And as to having a direction? Who has a direction at seventeen?'

My mind jumped to Mozart and Amy Winehouse but I didn't challenge her.

Maybe part of lending her the money was my way of saying thank you. For taking me along. For taking me seriously. And for helping me to speak. Speaking French with Lilou had opened a gigantic chamber in my head. When I didn't know a word, I tried another, or described what I wanted to say. My grammar was atrocious, but I'd get the hang of it eventually, she said. And anyway, she didn't seem to mind.

All that time wasted …

'Callum,' she'd asked earlier, 'why were you so reluctant to speak French?'

I tried to explain about not appearing inadequate, especially when Élodie and Florian were so effort-lessly at home in the world. 'I didn't want to look like an idiot. So, I kept my mouth shut.'

Lilou stared at me, exasperated. 'You are an idiot.'

'See?'

She rolled her eyes.

'It may seem obvious in retrospect, but I kind of panicked and went for silence. And then once I decided not to take the risk, it just … stuck.'

'You were stupid,' Lilou said. 'About everything, but particularly about that family. They are comfortable with their bourgeois lives, *plein d'assurance*, you understand? Full of self-confidence. That is not a thing to envy.'

I sighed. 'You don't know her. Élodie was different.'

Lilou rubbed her eyes. 'I don't know her, this is true, but I know her type. She's different for now, to annoy her mother. Nineteen years old, *à l'aise socialement*. And I know what you're thinking. "Why should someone perfect need to change?" But only an idiot would think that. She was born beautiful; she is graceful and confident. She will marry a bourgeois lawyer, identical to her lawyer brother and her lawyer father, and by the time she has one child, she will start dressing like her mother and thinking like her too. When she has two children, she will have no thoughts in her head that haven't already been thought ten times each day by everyone else in her village.'

This seemed grossly unfair. Just because a person was beautiful and from a small town didn't mean their soul was banal. But in a way, I knew what she meant. Being born beautiful was a guarantee that people would look at you, want to hang out with you, flirt with you, laugh at your jokes. Strangers found you loveable. The slightest generosity made you an angel. Act sullen, you were inscrutable. String a sentence together: fascinating. And if you said nothing at all: enigmatic.

The rest of us have to work at life.

As the temperature rose, stallholders hung damp tarps and home-made awnings over their wares to stop them from scorching. Lilou and I sat in the shelter of the doorway for the next hour in a companionable stupor. Every twenty minutes or so she got up and pressed the buzzer, but after the first tirade, there was no answer.

I mused over her appraisal of Élodie. 'How old are you, Lilou?'

She looked at her phone. 'Twenty-one tomorrow. If only it were today.'

'Why does it matter?'

'Because my godfather left me a small inheritance when he died, to come to me on my twenty-first birthday. By the time I get it, the audit will have discovered the missing money and I'll be arrested. It will be too late.'

'Then take mine,' I said, but she didn't answer.

We sat close together. And then she turned her face to mine and kissed me. Just like that. She kissed me, and I pulled back, shocked. 'What are you doing?'

'What do you think I'm doing?' She looked amused. 'Don't worry if you don't want to. You're too young for me anyway.'

I wanted to, so I kissed her back. It felt like tumbling slowly through space, like being stoned, dizzying, disorientating, very soft and impossibly sexy.

'Lilou!'

'*Oui, Callum?*'

'*Qu'est ce qu'on fait là?*'

She held her palms up and frowned as if trying to think of an answer. What are we doing here? She seemed not at all discomfited by the question.

'Is this because I offered to lend you money?' Christ, love was a minefield. Never mind sex.

'It's because I like you.'

'You do?'

'*Évidemment.*'

Huh. Funny how simple it seemed after a summer of hopeless longing. She liked me. I liked her. We kissed.

And just then, someone came out of the building and Lilou leaped up and grabbed the door before it slammed shut.

'We're in!' she called, triumphant.

I bolted after her up the stairs.

'I was serious, you know.' I panted, trying to catch up. 'You can have whatever money you need.'

She continued to take the stairs at a run.

We stopped on the fourth floor, found number 15, and she knocked.

No answer.

She paused, made a fist and banged as hard as she could. '*Ouvrez!*' she shouted, and then again. Until other people in the building began opening doors and shouting unrepeatable things at her.

At last we heard a click and the door opened a few inches. '*Putain! Qui est là?!*' demanded a surly voice from within.

It was Arnaud.

12

Arnaud was quick but Lilou was quicker.

When he saw who it was, he leaped forward to throw his body against the door but Lilou shoved her helmet in the crack and jammed it open, giving her leverage to force her way in. Arnaud fell back and I slipped in too, slamming the door shut behind me.

His mood had darkened since I saw him last. *Une maladie psychologique*, his mother had said. Of course, it *was* 6 a.m., and not everyone likes being woken at that hour by demands for money they no longer possess.

What transpired was a very heated conversation between Lilou and Arnaud that went something like this:

ARNAUD: Why are you chasing me around town?
Are you crazy?

LILOU: Why did you sneak out of the bar the
minute my back was turned? I need to pay the
money back today, Arnaud. It's important. Otherwise I'll lose my job. Do you think it's OK for me
to lose my job, just because I did you a favour?

ARNAUD (*sullen*): I didn't think there was such a
rush.

LILOU: But I've told you a hundred times! We
were meeting up expressly for you to give it back.
And what about the *hautbois*? And the Matisse?
You've graduated from petty crime to grand theft
larceny? What are you up to, you crazy bastard?

ARNAUD (*quietly triumphant*): I have a plan.

LILOU: A plan to steal from your own family and
friends?

ARNAUD: I didn't exactly steal either one. Particularly the oboe.

LILOU: You just borrowed it?

ARNAUD (*averts eyes*): It's complicated.

LILOU: I'm sure it is. I think you'd better tell me your plan.

ARNAUD: It's a surprise.

LILOU: I don't like surprises. And I definitely don't want to end up in jail as some sort of accessory to your crazy plan. But I will, Arnaud. I will. That money wasn't mine. If you don't pay me back, I am a thief. An embezzler.

ARNAUD: Well maybe you are one. I didn't ask you to steal it.

LILOU: You were desperate. You said it was life or death.

(ARNAUD *shrugs*.)

LILOU: You have nothing to say?

ARNAUD: There are more important issues than your two thousand euros.

LILOU: To you, maybe. But right now, it is life or death for *me*.

ARNAUD: Life or death? Don't be absurd.

LILOU: Simple for you to say that.

ARNAUD (*eerily calm*): The world will take notice of my plan.

LILOU: What does that mean?

ARNAUD: Wait and see.

LILOU: I can't. I need the money.

And here we were, back to the start again.

'*Les toilettes?*' I asked meekly, and Arnaud indicated a door next to the bedroom.

It was a small flat, with clothes draped on chairs, not much furniture, unopened mail on every surface, food containers discarded in heaps. None of the envelopes (most of which appeared to be unpaid bills) had Arnaud's name on them so I guessed he was just crashing here. Whoever did live here was never going to win Flat of the Year.

On the floor next to the bed were two plastic carrier bags. Not being the sort of person who made a habit of minding his own business, I looked into both.

Surprise.

'Arnaud,' I said, figuring sometimes the best approach is the direct one. 'What's this?' I held up two pieces of Harrison's oboe.

'Put them away!' he hissed.

In the other bag was a painting in a heavy wooden frame; various stickers on the back indicated the painting's provenance. It didn't matter how ignorant I was about art, I knew an expensive old frame when I saw one – heavy, carved, gilded. I lifted the painting carefully out of the bag and turned it over.

It was only a small painting, maybe thirty centimetres by thirty-five, but it collided with my brain like an asteroid. I stepped back in shock, unprepared for the brilliance of the colours, the oranges, golds and greens of the sky, the yellow and red grass, the vivid pink figures.

I didn't know much about art, true. But I couldn't look at this exuberant blast of colour without a feeling of exhilaration, a desire to laugh out loud. I looked away from it, looked back, felt a thrill of emotion. The landscape was joyous, a place of personal imaginary wonder created in the brain of a long-dead painter.

'It's a sketch,' Lilou told me. 'A preparatory painting for a much larger one called *Le Bonheur de Vivre*. You understand? The Joy of Life.'

'It's beautiful,' I said. But 'beautiful' was the wrong word. It was everything new and exciting I'd felt today, everything sharp and fresh, everything I'd never experienced before but hoped someday to feel. For the first time, I understood why people bothered with art, what it might add to life, the surge of happiness a picture might inspire.

I all at once understood what might cause someone to spend millions on a painting rather than a yacht or a house or a football team. Just looking at it for a moment created a place in my head, a place I could return to when I stopped believing in joy.

Perhaps it didn't have the same effect on Lilou.

She, after all, had seen it repeatedly over the years. But Lilou wasn't looking at the painting. 'For God's sake, Arnaud!'

Arnaud cast about anxiously, as if searching for spies. 'Shh. No one must know about this.' He spoke in a low voice to Lilou, and then turned to me. 'Put it back.'

Put it back in that ratty old plastic bag? The thought made me sick. To be honest, I could understand why he'd wanted to steal it. I felt exactly that impulse now, an overwhelming desire to take it home, to look at it whenever I liked.

Was he going sell it? You couldn't exactly sell a painting like this on the open market as if you'd found it in a ditch or behind the sofa, as if no one would wonder how you came to possess it. And as for the oboe, well, maybe it made a nice noise, but he could keep it as far as I was concerned. I'd have the painting.

'Arnaud.' Lilou spoke gently, coaxingly. 'Why don't

you give me the picture and I'll return it to your mother.'

'No.'

'The oboe then?'

'*Laisse moi.*'

'But you admire Harrison. And that oboe is his whole life.'

'It shouldn't be,' Arnaud said fiercely, a wild glint in his eye. 'There are more important things in life than playing music.'

That line again. And yes, obviously the world was full of things more important than Lilou's money and Harrison's oboe. But probably not at this precise moment, to Lilou and to Harrison.

She tried a different tack. 'You'll go to jail you know. You'll break your mother's heart.'

'I don't care what happens to me. And I don't want to discuss it further. You must leave now. Leave!'

Lilou hesitated. 'I'll go to the police.'

'You're best friends with the police now?' Arnaud

laughed. 'Just have a little patience. All will be revealed this afternoon, at the demo, in just a few hours. Be patient, Lilou, *mon chou*. Wait and see. Trust me.'

She stared Arnaud down like a bull facing a matador. He looked dishevelled and unhappy, had been sleeping in his clothes. At least he'd *been* asleep. I was jealous.

'It will all be fine,' he said. 'Better than fine. No more empty threats. They'll see I mean business.' His eyes blazed.

'Who's "they"?' I asked.

Arnaud didn't answer and Lilou glanced at me.

'I can't pay you back,' he said. 'Not right now anyway. I'm sorry, Lilou.'

'What is your plan, Arnaud? *Mon chéri?*' Her voice was softer, cajoling now.

'You'll see.' He looked at his watch. 'You haven't got long to wait.'

Lilou wasn't willing to give up on the money, but I was finding it hard to stay angry with Arnaud. He seemed so … nuts. I was, however, grossly worried about his plan, how much danger it represented, to how many people, and what he planned to do with the painting. The demo this afternoon was expected to attract tens of thousands of protesters.

I took her aside. 'You won't get your money,' I said in a low voice, surprised at how comprehensively she failed to grasp the obvious. 'Not now, maybe not ever. I think we should go.'

'But what about the painting? And Harrison? And my job?'

'We could just say we're taking the stuff with us? Grab the oboe and painting and back slowly towards the door? He seems pretty much out of it. We could try?'

Lilou nodded briefly.

Arnaud sat in the same position as before. 'Arnaud,' I began, speaking English. 'We're going to leave now and if you don't mind, we'll take the painting and the oboe with us. Is that OK?'

All at once there was something in his hand. At first I thought it was his phone but a second later I wasn't sure. When you see weapons on TV, they don't inspire much reaction. But in real life, the brutishness of what I thought I saw made me want to throw up.

Lilou gasped.

I reached out and took hold of her arm, to steady myself as much as anything. 'Let's go,' I said and, leaving the stolen goods, we backed silently towards the door. Arnaud remained motionless, staring at us.

We opened the door.

And ran, down the stairs, out on to the street, and around the corner just in case he was following us, which he wasn't.

Lilou looked genuinely shaken. 'There is something seriously not right with him, isn't there? I've got to talk to Jeannine.'

I nodded, at the same time wondering what his mother could do. What anyone could do. He wasn't exactly a child. 'Do we tell the police? You can't send him to jail. But what are his plans for the demo? Will he throw a bomb into the crowd? Is he dangerous? And how dangerous?'

Lilou paced. 'We could call the police and tell them we've found Harrison's stolen oboe and a priceless Matisse, which, by the way, has not been reported missing, belongs to his family, and is due to be inherited by the thief. I somehow don't think anyone would consider it urgent.'

Stated like that, I had to agree.

'And even if they took us seriously, Arnaud would have gone by the time they got here.'

'You think so?'

She nodded.

'Maybe we should just do as he says and wait a few hours.'

'For his great revelation?'

'Do you know the organisers? Could we tell them to keep an eye on him? Call the police if he gets up to anything?'

Lilou shook her head. 'Yes, I know the organisers. We both do. But the police aren't exactly thrilled about the demo to begin with. The atmosphere will be tense. We can't just phone them up and say, "We think one of our agitators has had *une dépression nerveuse* – would you mind taking a break to arrest him and take him to a place of safety in *une camisole de force*, a straitjacket, then return to throwing tear gas at the crowd?"'

'He seems so strange. Grandiose and depressed and irrational and …'

Lilou closed her eyes. '*Fou?*'

'Crazy' was a word I knew. 'Well, yes.'

She glanced at her phone. 'It's seven twenty-five. I'd better go and see Jeannine. Tell her about Arnaud, and that we've found the painting. Maybe she can do something about him.'

I longed to turn over responsibility for this whole complicated mess to someone old enough to solve it. Someone who wasn't me.

'The rally starts at four. I have things to organise beforehand. You phone Harrison. Tell him his oboe is safe.'

For now anyway.

'And wait here, I'll be quicker without you.' She reached in her pocket and took out ten euros. 'Have a coffee and something to eat in the meantime. I'll pick you up right here in an hour.'

I wasn't going to argue with food and drink. 'Go then,' I said. 'But take your two thousand euros. You might as well. Otherwise, we're wasting fate.'

'Wasting fate? C'est une expression anglaise?'

'No,' I said. 'But it feels like fate that we met.' I looked at her. 'So come on.' I opened the app and waited.

She hesitated.

'Like Meriam said, it's only money.'

'I will pay you back,' she said, and then read out her bank details.

Typing them in, I said, 'I trust you, Lilou.' She'd

already told me she was due to inherit money on her birthday. How much? I didn't really care. I trusted her. I trusted fate.

Ping!

'Magic,' she said, looking up at me with shining eyes. It was the first time since we'd met that she didn't look anxious. 'It's in my account.'

For a brief instant I panicked, felt that shudder of fear you experience when you think you've been scammed. But then I met her eyes and saw nothing I couldn't trust.

'I will pay you back,' she repeated, drawing a cross over her heart. And with a shrill whir from the bike, she was gone.

13

I did kiss Élodie. But if awards were given for the century's worst kiss, I'd have won hands down.

It all happened thanks to too much wine and a fair bit of subsequent miscommunication. I'm probably not the first person this has happened to.

We'd all gone to an opera by Purcell as part of the music festival. It was in English (this wasn't immediately obvious to me, as I'd never heard of Purcell), which was why they insisted I come along, though it didn't seem to matter as I couldn't hear any of the voices well enough to know what was being said. You could tell they were hugely puzzled by my inability to understand an opera in

English, but the stage was far away and the words unclear.

Christ, I thought. They'll imagine I don't speak any language at all now. That I'm some kind of wolf-child brought up in a forest who can only understand whimpers and grunts.

Élodie and Florian were, as usual, too polite to make me feel bad about not understanding English in addition to not understanding French, but they didn't have to go out of their way to make me feel bad: my default setting was bad-feeling.

The opera was outdoors, lit up against a beautiful Romanesque church. Blankets had been spread roughly in a fan-shape to eat picnics and listen to the music – blankets under the stars, baguettes, *fromage*, *beaucoup de vin*. Florian and Jacqui kissed, everyone else laughed and touched and flirted. It was sultry and warm and the moon was big. The air smelled of jasmine and bougainvillea. Everything was so sexy and French that for a moment I almost forgot how much I didn't belong with all those beautiful young people.

I lay looking at the stars and drinking from a glass that seemed miraculously to refill itself, thinking how almost nice it all was. Élodie lay near me propped up on her elbows, talking to some boy beside her, but her hair brushed my face when she laughed, and every once in a while she leaned into my shoulder, so I could feel the soft pressure of her breast against me. I couldn't bear how much I loved her. I knew she was playing with me, while pretending not to, and the wine was flirting with my brain. So that when she leaned to pass the bottle to the boy on the other side of me, all I needed to do was lift my head a few inches and my lips would be touching her lips.

So that's what I did.

She drew back as if burned, with an expression that I will never forget, of something like disgust. It was so awful it made actual tears spring to my eyes. I turned my face away to pretend it hadn't happened, and though she quickly changed her expression into one of teasing affection, it was too late.

Half a minute later she levered herself up off the ground with infinite casualness and walked over to the other side of the group, folding her legs neatly under her like a whippet and half reclining with her customary sweet smile, charming the boys around her. She didn't come within an arm's length of me for the rest of my stay with the family. I felt humiliated and ashamed.

And yet, since last night, nothing that had happened this summer seemed so bad. A kiss, an attractive bourgeois family, a life in the beautiful French countryside with good music and nice clothes. I no longer cared. I had emerged from the past into a present where life seemed sharp and real and a painting could make you feel the joy of life.

I stared down at Lilou's ten euros. It would cover a Métro ticket to Gare du Nord with maybe enough left over for a coffee. Or I could trust Lilou to come back, and order breakfast.

Breakfast won, by a mile. I entered the nearest café, ordered *un café crème* and a *jambon-beurre*, devouring both in a trance of happy greed. Then, with caffeine and carb courage powering through my veins, I switched on my phone, recoiling as WhatsApp exploded in a wild barrage of pings. My parents. Moe. My parents. Moe. European Adventures Abroad. One friend. Another. My parents again. And again. And again. Each wondering if I was dead or alive, had been murdered or kidnapped, and if not, why the hell wasn't I answering my phone?

To my horror, the charge hovered at two per cent. NO!

I checked the time (07:55) and began frantically texting Harrison – when the screen went black. A deep gloom descended on me. Without Lilou and the motorbike and the mad chase across Paris, there was nothing to distract me from my predicament. Lost and alone. Not to mention broke. Just to confirm the final humiliation, I found a bank and tried withdrawing fifty euros on my card, but it hummed for a bit and then read TRANSACTION REFUSÉE – all in caps, for emphasis, like telling a dog 'no!' in a loud, firm voice. So that was it, no more money.

So, I waited. Twenty minutes. Forty. I wandered around the market looking for a toilet, returning to the place Lilou had left me, or at least the place I was pretty sure she'd left me – everything looked more or less the same to me here and most of the tiny streets weren't marked.

I sat down in a sheltered corner of La Maison des Épices, in wherever it was I was, surrounded by small mountains of cumin, nutmeg and black pepper, and fell instantly asleep, my cheek against a brick wall covered in graffiti, the roof offering half-shade from the sun that threatened to turn me to dust.

I half woke. Checked my phone.

Still dead.

How long had I been asleep? One hour? Two? Here I was out past the *périphérique*, in a suburb of Paris whose name I couldn't remember with no money, no friends, no charge on my phone. No Lilou.

A lifetime ago I'd been dozing peacefully through a concert and drinking wine at Le Canard but now I reconciled myself to the fact that Lilou was not coming back. She'd obviously decided to take the money and run, and though I felt awful about this – awful that I'd misjudged her so completely, that our night of adventure had all been some kind of ruse to get me to part with my cash, that all the sympathy and connection I'd felt between us had been false – it was not unexpected.

I could have cried.

But I didn't.

The disappointment felt bad, but also familiar, and I mentally kicked myself for expecting more. Moping wasn't going to help. I had to get to Gare du

Nord, charge my phone, contact my parents and beg them to send me a ticket. Once I was home, they could tell me at length and in great detail how useless I was.

Something to look forward to.

As with all great things, my adventure had come to an end. No point putting a brave face on it. Thirst was my overwhelming concern just now, so I used the remains of my ten euros to buy a bottle of water, and asked the guy selling it which way it was to Gare du Nord.

'*Là-bas,*' he said pointing vaguely west. But when it became obvious I would be walking, he changed tack, shook a forbidding finger and added, '*Mais trop chaud, trop loin!*' Too hot! Too far! I thanked him and set off in roughly the direction he'd indicated. He stood watching for some time with consternation. I waved back in a reassuring 'I like long walks in the killing heat' sort of way, but I could still see his lips moving, muttering '*Trop chaud, trop loin*' like a curse.

It was time for me to go. I couldn't stick around waiting for everyone's life to be sorted out. At this rate, it would take years. And anyway, none of these people was my responsibility. I pushed Lilou out of my head.

The heat crushed everything: colour, movement, business and pleasure. Paris felt defeated. An awful weariness drained the life out of my surroundings. I'd run out of options. I was down and out, burned-out, sunburned, alone. I'd given a fabulous con-woman all my money. I'd chased all over Paris looking for the guy who (thanks to me) stole my cousin's oboe, but finding it hadn't seemed to help.

To say I wasn't looking forward to the next conversation with my parents was putting it mildly. But in the end, I knew they would send me a ticket. They wouldn't condemn me to a career as a rent boy on the streets of Paris, no matter how annoyed they were.

The time had come to go home.

14

Trudging through the fiery streets in a general westerly direction, it wasn't long before I realised that if I didn't sit down soon, I would die of heatstroke. So, I followed a handful of Dutch tourists and walked through the gate of what turned out to be a cemetery, an important cemetery judging by the scale of it, with big trees, huge monuments and shady corners. Perfect, I thought. I can rest a few minutes here.

The cemetery was cooler than the streets, with row after row of mausoleums, tiny chapels, great marble statues and, best of all, shade trees. The overall effect was of a sprawling village with deserted streets and quaint little homes where no one ever came round for tea. Great stone and wooden front doors led to crypts, some decorated with ornate angels and marble women mourning the deceased, some with cherubs or dogs or lions guarding the entrance.

Queues of red-faced foreigners trailed after tour leaders waving droopy little flags. Nearly everyone wore headsets so they could hear fascinating facts about the dead in their own language. Most looked as if they'd be a lot happier in the south of France with a cocktail, dangling their feet in a pool. No judgement intended. I would too.

A ridiculous number of them videoed everything they saw, and I tried to imagine how the conversations at home would go, along the lines of 'You want to see my forty-eight-minute video of a cemetery in Paris?'

To which the only possible answer was, 'I'd rather die.'

As the tourists straggled from dead famous person to dead famous person, I found a nondescript grave off the beaten track, next to a tree, behind which I had a pee as quickly and discreetly as possible. Then I sat down in the shade and tried resting my head on the cool white marble, but even the marble was warm. My mausoleum housed an extended family of about a dozen of the departed, including a number of small children, a patriarch who had lived to eighty-eight, and two women ten years apart who'd entered this special village at about the right age to have died giving birth, or attempting to.

I felt I could smell the dead, an earthy, musty odour like the inside of an abandoned barn. But maybe it was just the heat.

A night on the back of Lilou's motorbike had coated me in dust, now mixed with sweat on a base of sunburn. I was still desperately thirsty and very sorry for myself, plotting how I could steal another bottle of water out of some unsuspecting tourist's bag while he adjusted his selfie-stick.

With some irony (given recent events), I realised I didn't have the nerve.

Too thirsty to do anything but drowse in a kind of half-conscious torpor, I sat for an hour or two, at last hauling myself upright and heading for the cemetery exit, where gigantic, air-conditioned coaches pulled in to collect their tourist cargo. For a moment I stood rooted, fantasizing about slipping aboard a luxury coach at random and hitching a ride to wherever it was headed. Just to sit somewhere cool.

Would I doze off and wake up in Seoul? It was worth the risk.

A crowd of mostly overweight Americans with cowboy hats and the occasional MAGA cap (did Trump voters own passports?) queued politely as their tour guide handed out cardboard lunch boxes and bottles of water. My homeless-foreigner-in-Paris look caused the guide to call out 'Hey, kid!' and toss me a plastic bottle. It was ice cold and I didn't know whether to pour it on my head or drink it.

'Thank you,' I called back. 'Really!'

'Hey! Great accent!' The guide beckoned me over. 'You English?'

I nodded.

'On your own?'

'It's kind of a long story.' I sighed. 'I gave all my money to a girl who ditched me and now I'm broke.'

'Holy shit!' the guy said. 'That's rotten! French girl?' His look told me I couldn't trust foreigners, especially foreign women, and I was a darn fool for thinking I could.

I answered his question with a sad frown and a pathetic nod. Looking pathetic was not difficult. I was, in fact, pathetic.

'Hey, kid, you gotta watch out for French girls, everyone knows that.'

'Too late,' I said, feeling a bit guilty about lumping Lilou in with all those ruthless Mata Haris. On the other hand, she had taken my money and abandoned me. 'Look,' I said, 'I'm sure it's totally against the rules, but I might die if I have to walk any further, and with all my money gone I'm kind of stuck. I don't suppose you could give me a lift? I don't really care where you're going.'

'Well …' He pronounced it *Waaay-ehll*, making the single syllable last about three and a half minutes.

'I'm not one to beg,' I said, which was not remotely true.

'*Waaay-ehll* …' he said again. 'I'm responsible for this group but I can't see how anyone'd give two figs if you caught a lift with us to Notre Dame.' He pronounced it *No-der Day-um*. 'That direction OK by you?'

'Close enough.'

'Pretty darn long walk in this heat,' the guy said, the American version of *trop chaud, trop loin*, and held out his hand. 'Mike.'

'Callum,' I replied, taking hold of it slightly too enthusiastically with both hands, to express gratitude and as much affection as if he'd been Dr Livingstone, I presume. 'Thank you for saving my life, Mike.'

'No problem. Just sit up front with me and don't tell anyone you're a stowaway. Company's funny about insurance.'

I could do that.

The interior of the coach was about twenty-five degrees cooler than the world outside and I sank into the big reclining faux-leather seat, my eyes rolled-back with bliss. As the members of the tour group began climbing back aboard, Mike roll-called a long list of names. 'Armstrong, Baker, Barnett, Crouch, Dawson, Ellis, Fracker ...' Occasionally Mike would pause and call 'Do I have two of you?' for the married couples.

The overall vibe was friendly and they didn't particularly strike me as the sort of people who'd firebomb abortion clinics, but looks can be deceptive.

Everyone was too happy to be sitting down in the Arctic to notice me.

'All aboard?' Mike called.

A few enthusiasts responded 'You betcha!' and 'Yeee-haw!' and at last the driver climbed into his huge driver's seat, shut the doors, threw us into reverse, and off we set in a great cloud of toxic diesel fumes.

Until today, cruising through Paris in a gigantic coach filled with Trump voters would have filled me with horror. But compared to wandering lost through the heat, this was paradise.

By the time Mike returned to the seat next to mine, I'd plugged in my phone and dozed off.

15

I woke to the sight of the passengers all crowded over on my side of the bus, and in my semi-conscious state I figured we must be driving past the Mona Lisa or the Taj Mahal to make them all take such a keen interest in the outside world.

'Hey,' said Mike. 'Look at that crazy girl! What the heck is she up to?'

An innocent enough question. I struggled to sit up and focus. We were stopped at a red light and at first I couldn't see anything but an ordinary street scene with cars, shops, pedestrians, a few cyclists and scooters. And then I noticed the motorbike. And the girl on the motorbike. Looking straight in the window at me. Shouting my name.

'CALLLUMMM!'

'Oh bloody hell,' I said.

'Language, young man,' said Mike. 'Does she know you? Do you know each other?'

I wondered what the chances of a random French girl calling my name were.

'She's the one who took my money,' I said, feeling somewhat disingenuous, considering she didn't appear to be avoiding me.

'Well, in that case I'd say it's pretty darn lucky you found her,' he said, and before I could take action, he'd opened the door, dashed out into traffic and grabbed Lilou by the arm. He made a gigantic show of waving and pointing at me, as if she hadn't already spotted my profile pressed drooling against the window of a tour bus full of Texans.

I was overjoyed to see Lilou again but couldn't quite shake the feeling that I was living in the Matrix.

Or as Moe would have put it, we are all but a dream in the eye of God.

Shut up, Moe.

While all this swirled through my brain, Lilou and Mike were headed back to the bus. The driver opened the door and in she trotted, looking simultaneously relieved and cross. She'd left her bike propped up in the middle of traffic.

'Cal-lum, Cal-lum,' a desultory chant started at the back of the coach and died out just as soon.

Squaring up to me, she said, loudly, 'Are you deaf?'

'I was just going to—'

'When I came back you'd gone.'

'You said one hour.'

'I was delayed.'

'By two hours?'

'Twenty minutes, actually. And where were you?'

To be honest, I'm not entirely sure.

Lilou frowned. 'I wasn't very late. You moved.'

'I'm too tired to argue,' I said, because I was too tired to argue.

All around us the traffic was hooting, people leaned on horns, furious drivers shouted obscenities out of windows. The bus driver, American and ever polite, turned to Lilou and said, 'Excuse me, miss, but I'm afraid you'll have to get off the bus now.'

She stood her ground, facing me. 'Are you coming?'

'Get off the bus!' called someone a few rows back.

'Get off the bus!' chimed in someone from the back.

'Get off the bus, get off the bus!' This time the chant took hold.

Mike looked at me. 'Sorry, Cal, but you're turning out to be way more trouble than you're worth.'

And he stood up to let me pass, which I did promptly, because aside from a petty argument about who was or was not where they should have been and why, I was hugely relieved to see Lilou and, with the possible exception of the air conditioning, not at all unhappy to leave the mobile luxury hotel of the Texans.

The 'get-off' chant faded as I descended the staircase, but not before I heard a few people segue to 'Good luck! Good luck!' with one lone voice muttering 'Fuck off! Fuck off!', which had an irate Mike on his feet, striding to the back of the coach, looking for the culprit.

For a minute, the hot air outside felt amazing; the bus had been much too cold after all night on the steaming streets. I'm sure I'd heard you could get pneumonia from exposure to violent changes of temperature.

Lilou handed me my helmet and I took it just as if there'd been no break in our association. I braced against the top-box as we accelerated away, this time to escape the lynch mob that had emerged from a six-minute traffic jam. Maybe there were people on their way to hospital with heatstroke or late for world climate summits and I felt guilty about those people, but everyone else could stuff it.

'Where are we going?' I shouted, which by now could have been my theme tune, but she didn't hear/ ignored me, which could have been hers.

16

Within a few minutes we'd reached Harrison's flat. I wished I'd asked Mike for one of the leftover lunch boxes as I was hungry again. It had been hours since my breakfast baguette.

We rang the bell and trudged up the stairs, my mind plodding slowly in circles like a donkey hooked to the crank of a well. What would I say to him? *So, the guy I introduced you to did in fact steal your oboe and I was at a certain point today holding it in my hand, but for various reasons, possibly involving drugs, mental instability and a lethal weapon, I couldn't recover it for you. Sorry about that.*

The door flew open.

'Hello, Callum,' said Harrison. And to Lilou, 'Hello, Callum's friend, I'm afraid I don't remember your name. I'm glad you're still alive, Callum. Your disappearance was … unforeseen. Your family has been hounding me non-stop to find you and send forensic evidence that you are still alive, which I have, sadly, been unable to do. Do you ever answer your phone or is it just for decoration?'

'I ran out of charge.'

'Ah.' And then to Lilou, 'Are you part of the gang that stole my oboe?'

She looked annoyed, planted her hands on her hips and shook her head. '*Pas du tout.*'

He nodded. 'I've told the police that my oboe was stolen and all three witnesses at the table disappeared at once. They found this somewhat suspicious, so either they'll issue a warrant for your arrest or mark me in their records as a foreign fantas-ist with delusions of victimhood.' He turned back to me. 'Sorry, Callum, but you have to admit your behaviour has been somewhat …' He paused, no doubt searching for a better word than 'weird'. 'Weird.'

I flipped back through all the goings-on since I'd met him and had to agree. 'Yes,' I said, 'but this is not what it looks like.'

'What does it look like?' Harrison asked. 'A medium-sized plane crash? All I know is that my oboe is gone and the insurance company is suspicious as hell.'

'Well …' I took a deep breath. 'So, the guy I introduced you to did, in fact, steal your oboe and I was at a certain point today holding it in my hand, but for various reasons, possibly involving drugs, mental instability and a lethal weapon, I couldn't recover it for you. I am sorry. Truly. You probably wish you'd never met me.'

'Oh, I definitely wish that,' Harrison said. 'You've ruined my life.'

Bit strong, surely?

'You don't get it,' he said. 'It's almost impossible to make a living playing the oboe *before* it's stolen. The practice, the rehearsals, but above all, the reeds.'

'Huh?' I had to suppress a mental picture of a marsh full of bulrushes.

'The reeds,' Harrison said slowly, as if speaking to the village idiot. 'You blow through them. Across them. It takes hours to make double reeds that work. And then when you've perfected a reed, shaped it and scraped it millimetre by millimetre until the sound it produces is exactly right, then you play a single piece of music, maybe even a few phrases or a few notes, and hey presto, it no longer works. And you have to start all over again. It's soul destroying.'

'That's tough,' I agreed. 'But would you say it's my fault?'

He ignored me. 'There's no rhyme or reason as to why the one I made on Tuesday is perfect and the one I made on Wednesday buzzes.'

'Why would anyone choose to play an instrument

like that?' I asked. 'I mean, no offence, but it's not like it sounds any better than all those instruments that aren't nearly so exasperating to play.' To me this seemed a perfectly reasonable question.

'You have a point,' said Harrison gloomily. 'It's impossible to play, the reeds are impossible to make. It has too many holes, each hole plays too many notes and if one key, one minute section of a rod, changes shape, gets bumped, expands or bends even a fraction of a millimetre due to, I don't know, atmospheric disturbance, the whole thing goes wrong and the sound is ruined. It's a life of total heartbreak.'

'Gosh,' I said, shaking my head like I cared. 'Still, the concert sounded nice.' I was trying to be helpful. What attracted people to such a futile existence?

'Nice?' Harrison's despond deepened. 'Gee, thanks very much.'

'Much better than nice,' Lilou said, frowning at me. 'Outstanding.'

'Plus, every oboe costs a fortune to make. And to

buy. A good violin can last five hundred years. A good oboe? Ten. Tops.'

'That's terrible.' It was unbearably hot in his flat and I was pretty sure I smelled bad. It was the sort of weather that required hourly cold showers and I'd been sweating for what felt like weeks. Though obviously I had sympathy for Harrison, I didn't care very much about his plight, especially as you could argue that he had brought it on himself, having voluntarily chosen to play the oboe. 'And I'm very, very sorry I introduced you to a notorious oboe thief.'

He held a finger up, requesting that I hold off on my apology. There was more to say about the misery of his life, and he was going to say it if it killed him. 'So, I practise four hours each day. I work on my reeds for another few hours, I practise and rehearse and play concerts. But none of it adds up. The concerts don't pay enough because I'm not famous enough, so no one hires me to play the really important gigs but the work to prepare is exactly the same as if I were playing Lincoln Center every night. And with all that, there's no time to have a life. My girlfriend was great but she left me. She said I forgot her birthday.'

'Did you?' Remembering your partner's birthday struck me as the lowest bar in a relationship.

'I had a concert. It paid less than a hundred euros. I could have bought her a present if I hadn't needed the money for food.'

Ah.

Harrison sighed. 'It's a beautiful instrument but a terrible life. And the money doesn't begin to compensate.'

The money. I had a funny feeling that at last we were getting somewhere. 'So, what do you do about it? Get another job? Teach?'

'In my spare time? Oh sure.'

I looked at Harrison. He looked back at me with an odd expression. Misery, yes. But also – guilt.

Why guilt?

My brain slowly cranked to life like a mechanical bear waking from a long hibernation.

So, you spend your entire life studying and honing your talent in a relentless struggle to advance, to make enough money to live, one step forward, two steps back. You're good, you're talented – unusually talented even – but mainly you work hard. Hardly anyone has a clue how much hard work goes into what you do. Mostly they say (usually with some resentment) how lucky you are to be born with a God-given talent – as if it just arrived one day, like the ability to use a spoon. But you're not the only talented, hardworking musician around, there are lots of you, and you're all in competition for relatively few high-profile opportunities to perform, with little real chance of recognition, except within your equally overworked, fanatical cohort. Oh, and did we mention that playing classical music, even to a far-above-average standard, doesn't pay as well as the average supermarket warehouse manager? So, what do you do to get ahead of the financial abyss?

My brain spun.

Maybe, I thought with infinite slowness, *maybe* your long-lost cousin accidentally introduces you to a mentally unstable semi-criminal musician willing to commit fraud.

Maybe, after a long chat in a bar late at night, your new friend suggests that the two of you fake a heist.

Or *maybe* the thought has occurred to you before.

Maybe it's *you* who raises the subject.

Maybe you allow/encourage this guy to walk out of the bar with your very valuable instrument, at which point you plan to claim it's been stolen, inform the police, file for the (substantial) insurance money, and use it to pay your debts. Then your criminal friend kindly returns your oboe the next day when no one's looking, you cut him in on the insurance payout, and eventually go back to playing, claiming you've bought a new oboe with the insurance money and hope nobody notices.

I've always been told I have a vivid imagination, but there was something about the neat way this story formed in my head and pulled together so many loose ends that made me think *maybe*, just *maybe*, it might be true.

I looked at Harrison. He looked back at me. Lilou looked at us both. Nobody said a word.

'I have a theory,' I said at last. 'It's a little far-fetched – in fact it's very far-fetched. If everything that happened lately hadn't confused me so much, I might never have put all these pieces together and come up with the world's most unlikely scenario. But given the oddness of the circumstances, I think you should humour me.'

Harrison had started to look twitchy. Lilou was staring at me with interest.

'Here's my theory,' I said. 'Let me know what you think of it. I may be way off base.' I paused. 'And then again, I may not be.'

I took a deep breath.

'Let's just imagine you start chatting with Arnaud at the bar. You tell him your oboe sob story and he's incredibly sympathetic. He thinks you're a musical genius, and also, he needs money too.'

'Badly,' Lilou interjected. 'He needs money badly.'

I nodded. 'You have a couple of drinks, and one of you comes up with a brilliant idea. What if you fake a heist? What if Arnaud "steals" your oboe on the understanding that he takes a cut of the insurance payout. You have a couple more drinks and you think this might be the best idea you've ever had.'

'Also, it's hot,' Lilou interjected. 'And everyone's getting drunker than usual.'

Once more I nodded. 'So you make an agreement and then Arnaud discreetly removes the oboe from the case at your feet, says goodbye and disappears from the bar, promising he'll bring it back sometime the next day. You report the theft to the police who, let's face it, have bigger fish to fry than oboe abduction, so they – cheerfully and without much scrutiny – write a report that you can pass on to the insurance company. Having only known Arnaud for a few hours, you assume – erroneously, and you might want to have a chat with Lilou about that – that he's a decent guy and will stick to his part of the bargain, returning your oboe the next day. At which point all the people who didn't care that much about the heist to begin with won't care about it at all.'

Lilou gasped. 'This is a set-up?'

The more I spoke it out loud, the more the story made perfect sense. 'Arnaud planned to pay Lilou back with his cut of the insurance money.' I turned to Harrison. 'And everyone present would have lived happily ever after. Except Lilou, for whom the pay-back would have come too late. And except Harrison, when it turned out that your weakest link – that is Arnaud by a country mile – decides he doesn't feel like returning the oboe after all. Who knows why? Maybe he has some crackpot plan to make a big splash at the climate demo later this afternoon and it's not uppermost on his list of priorities. Maybe he just forgot.'

I paused. Lilou looked almost dazed with shock.

Harrison failed to make eye contact with either of us. He's suddenly looking a lot like a guy who'd like to turn time back about sixteen hours and take a sobriety pledge before he arrives at Le Canard.

Where was I?

Oh yes. 'So, your new best friend, the fake criminal, turns out, surprise surprise, to be an *actual* criminal. Or possibly just a bit of a loose cannon. Or mentally unstable. Who could possibly have guessed that? And you turn out to be the mastermind of an insurance swindle gone wrong. Which, I can only guess, is not a good look in the upper echelons of the classical music world.'

Lilou stared at Harrison. 'I don't know who's crazier, you or Arnaud.'

Harrison drooped. 'It's still early. He might be on his way over with it now.'

'Only he's not,' I said. 'As far as I can tell, he's forgotten all about you, and if you ever see your oboe again it will be the surprise of the century.'

'Oh dear,' said Lilou in English.

'But hang on,' I said, thinking about all this. 'Is insurance fraud really that easy? If so, I don't know why anyone bothers getting a real job. I mean, doesn't your oboe have a serial number that someone might consider checking?'

Nobody spoke.

'And also, this was not exactly a long-term solution, was it? I mean, how much could an oboe possibly be worth anyway? What's the maker's name? I never heard of Stradivarius making wind instruments.'

'Howarth,' mumbled Harrison. 'Fifteen grand.'

Huh.

All the puzzle pieces jiggled and joggled, and then,

with a bit of rudimentary dexterity, they all lined up. Like the lemons on a slot machine. Like the colours on a Rubik's cube. Like magic.

I looked at my cousin. 'You could go to jail, Harrison.'

He nodded wretchedly. 'I know. I wish I'd never met Arnaud.'

'Hang on,' Lilou said. 'Didn't you say you reported *me* to the police, just for leaving the bar at the same time as Arnaud? Which makes me a false accessory to your stupid crime on the basis of entirely circumstantial evidence?'

'Probably,' said Harrison gloomily.

'Not entirely circumstantial,' I offer. 'You left the bar to go after Arnaud, for another reason entirely. Also with criminal overtones.'

'He reported your disappearance too,' Lilou pointed out.

'So, I'll go to jail with you.' I hoped we'd get to share a cell.

'I'd be happy to see you both incarcerated,' Harrison said.

I felt a bit annoyed now. 'It's not like I forced you to come up with the stupidest illegal money-making scheme in history, Harrison. And even if I did, which I didn't, you were the one who decided to act on it.'

There was a long, unhappy silence.

'I *really* wish I'd never met you,' my cousin said.

The feeling was entirely mutual.

17

There's nothing worse than people you know having squishy sex in the bed next to yours, especially when the gap between the beds is less than a metre.

And the thing is, Jacqui stayed after they were done (the muffled but not at all silent orgasms), so there was endless rustling and murmuring through-out the night until she snuck off at about 6 a.m. to the room she was supposed to share with Élodie when she stayed over, with no one (I didn't count) the wiser. I couldn't bear to look at Florian after hearing his love language, which mainly consisted of whis-pered '*Ah, oui, oui, comme ça, oui, oui, chérie, oui, baise-moi.*'

Occasionally it occurred to me that I could join in, be the phantom disembodied hand that appeared in the mix when no one was paying attention. This thought served mainly to pass the time while wishing I'd paid more for my noise-cancelling headphones. Don't worry, by the way. I didn't do it. Too creepy.

Did anyone care what they were doing and where she slept? Probably not. The parents no doubt considered my presence insurance against exactly what was going on. And after all, they were seventeen and sixteen, comfortably in line with the age of consent in France.

'Give me Arnaud's address,' Harrison was saying. 'I'm going to get my oboe back.'

'He's not in a good way,' Lilou said.

And more likely to bludgeon you to death than return it.

'He's also got a stolen Matisse and a weapon and some kind of plan he keeps talking about. Which adds up to …' She paused, sighed. 'Something. Who knows what.'

'I don't care if it's a bad idea,' Harrison said. 'This is life or death.'

It patently was *not* life or death.

Harrison looked as if he might cry. 'It's a total disaster. How can I play concerts—'

'Due to your –' I made air quotes – '*stolen oboe*? Which, because you called the police and reported it to the insurance company, you can't suddenly pretend to have found in the pocket of an old jacket?'

'Oh, for God's sake.' Lilou had lost patience. 'Tell the police it was all a mistake. Your wife took it home, your friend left it in the dressing room, you woke up and it was all a dream. Embrace poverty and get back to your pathetic little life making reeds—'

'Double reeds,' Harrison muttered.

'… *double* reeds for your stupid oboe and stop complaining.' Lilou shook her head. 'There are much bigger problems in the world,' she said. 'Believe me.'

You could tell she and Harrison were never going to hit it off.

'That's all well and good,' Harrison said, 'but your friend Arnaud is still in possession of it. So technically speaking, it is still stolen.'

Accidentally real-stolen as opposed to fake-stolen.

'Go and get it then,' Lilou said. 'It's worth a try.' And she gave him the address. 'The concierge might give him the code if he's not there.'

Lilou turned to me. 'Now that we've solved at least some of the mystery, I think you should come back to my flat, get cleaned up, rest for half an hour, then call your father and ask him to buy you a ticket to London. Go back to your old life, the one before all these idiot French people made you the star of your own *comédie loufoque*. I don't know how to translate that.'

'Screwball comedy,' Harrison volunteered, and then turned to me. 'And maybe you could not tell your family about …' He waved his hands vaguely around the room, indicating everyone in it and, presumably also, this point in history.

'Of course,' I said, because I'd shake hands with Putin right now for a shower and half an hour's sleep.

'You get a train back to London and I will go to my demo and hope Arnaud has calmed down,' she said, and then turning to Harrison: 'And then if you have no success with Arnaud today, hopefully I can get your oboe back. OK?'

'OK.'

'Excellent. Let's go.'

For all Élodie's adorable female tricks and tropes, for all that she smelled like rare flowers, draped herself in flimsy scraps of cotton and silk, for all that her smile was enigmatic, that her eyes beckoned you closer, for all that she would seduce you while pretending to do anything but – for all *that*, Élodie could not hold even the tiniest of tiny candles to Lilou in her white jeans and leather boots, the fringe that nearly hid her eyes, her kindness, her unwillingness to suffer fools, her energy, her resolve.

Élodie was maddening, but Lilou was formidable,

in the English sense of being a formidable opponent, and in the French sense of being just plain amazing. She was brave and bold, forthright and strong, *magnifique et sublime. For-mi-DA-ble.*

Harrison left us for the Métro. I clambered aboard the bike and Lilou twisted to face me. 'You saved my life today, Callum. The money is back in the work account with no one the wiser. I've felt sick with fear for an entire month and now I'm saved.' She took hold of my hand. 'Do you have any idea how grateful I am? I was reconciled to losing everything: my job, my apartment, my whole life. I can breathe again, thanks to you.'

I felt suddenly shy, anxious to deflect the attention. 'All that stress, because of Arnaud.'

She shook her head firmly. '*Non.* It was not Arnaud's fault,' she said. 'It was mine. I should not have touched that money, for anyone. Not for the Pope, not for Mother Teresa. It didn't belong to me, and it was entirely wrong that I took it. I had some big idea that I could save Arnaud from his drug-dealer criminal friends. He promised the money could save him. But it couldn't.'

'You cared about him.'

'It was still wrong. You can't save people. It's pure self-regard to think you can.' She turned around and started the bike.

As I pulled on my helmet, threaded the strap through the D-ring, and braced to set off, I thought: *But you saved me.*

18

I was wide awake on the back of a motorbike dreaming about food.

It had to be nearly three by now and I dreamed of a gigantic omelette, something with Gruyère and spinach and loads of cream and eggs. Or failing that, a great slab of rustic pâté, a baton or two and some gherkins. And maybe a *tarte au citron* as big as my—

Lilou pulled over to the side of the road and cut the engine.

'*Tu es sûr?*'

Bluetooth. I wished I could hear.

'Ah-huh.'

Pause.

'*Oui.*' Sigh. '*OK. J'arrive.*' She turned round to me. 'I'm sorry, Callum. Arnaud's turned up at Les Invalides. We need to go.'

Bloody Arnaud. If he'd planned a meticulous campaign expressly to prevent me from getting half an hour's sleep, it couldn't have been more successful.

Lilou turned west and headed along the river towards the Eiffel Tower. I'd seen glimpses of it the night before, lit up golden in the night, but this was something altogether different. It was daytime, and as we approached Les Invalides, it looked so ridiculously, magnificently French. Tears burned in my eyes.

Oh get a grip, I told myself.

As we drew closer, I noticed a gradually increasing number of people on the street, mostly young. First handfuls, then groups, then crowds. Big demonstrations had also been planned for Lyons and Marseilles, but it seemed that everyone in Paris was out on the streets today.

We arrived on a side street near Les Invalides across from what appeared to be the demo head-quarters. Lilou stopped her bike. Organisers in black T-shirts held loudhailers and microphones; rock music played. The atmosphere was more like a festival than a demo, but a few metres away, people unrolled banners in preparation: *JUSTICE CLIMATIQUE, INDIGNEZ-VOUS*, and *VOTEZ 'OUI' AUX IMPÔTS*.

A makeshift platform had been set up in the middle of Les Invalides. In long rows two-deep, the police stood stock-still with black reflective helmets and riot shields, like shock troopers from *Star Wars*. So far, they merely watched.

'Look,' said Lilou, pointing.

I looked.

A huge digital thermometer recorded the current temperature, followed by the words *C'EST TROP*. Currently, it read 45 degrees. Ten or fifteen people milled about on the platform in front of the billboard. I recognised Saïd, who had sent us to Meriam.

And Arnaud.

He stood out from the others on stage due to a certain nervous energy, an aura of wrongness. His gait was jerky, he stared rigidly out into the crowd; as alone as if he'd been standing in a spotlight. He didn't speak a word to any of his compatriots. It was impossible to define exactly why his mere presence, nearly a football-pitch distance away, made me so uneasy.

Lilou secured the bike and we pushed into the crowd, which closed back around us until we could barely move in any direction. Speakers on the platform boomed out rousing calls to action; organisers, guests and Green politicians made appeals. It was a typical rally warm-up – the heavy hitters waited in the wings till the crowd was at peak capacity. At the edges of the demo, medical teams stood by; people were already succumbing to the heat.

It was too hot for violence, too hot, almost, for chanting and cheering. Everything seemed heavy and inert.

And then Arnaud took the stage.

'*Bonjour, mes amis,*' he boomed into the microphone. '*Aujourd'hui, je suis là pour vous dire à tous …*' He spoke in French but I understood every word. '*I am here today to tell you all that the people who make our laws do not understand what this climate crisis means — to us, to our children, to future generations. Our government pretends to act, they pass laws, they take steps, but their steps are too small and too slow.*'

There was a scattering of applause.

'*Nos gouvernements ne peuvent pas continuer … Our governments cannot continue to ignore the reality of our planet. There is no hiding from Armageddon. We must make our voices heard. Action requires personal sacrifice.*'

He paused for a moment, and Lilou and I looked

at each other. Was this his big idea – personal sacrifice? What did that mean exactly?

And then Arnaud turned around, rustled about in a pile of boxes at the rear of the stage and pulled out a large plastic bag. It was the size and shape of the Matisse canvas, but when he reached into it, what he pulled out was a stack of greenish-blue paper. Oblong. The size and shape of banknotes. They were banknotes, in fact, fistfuls of them. He scattered them around his feet like kindling, where they ruffled gently in the faint breeze, then he reached into the bag for more.

As he arranged the euros, a hot gust of wind caught a few and began swirling them off the platform. It took the crowd a beat or two before first one person, then another and another began to understand what was happening. They milled about, cheerfully at first, then more furiously, leaping and grabbing at twenty-euro notes, shouting and fighting to be first to reach them. Slowly, what was happening filtered back through the crowd, to the people at the outer edges and the back, but Arnaud barely noticed. He was too busy with a bottle of wine he had removed from his bag. Wine? What the hell was he up to?

Some in the crowd were laughing and I could understand why – the whole scene seemed bonkers, money flying through the air, the man on stage making doomsday pronouncements and then producing a bottle of wine like some demented clown.

I turned to look at Lilou, but she had already left my side and was pushing through the packed crowd, grimly determined to reach the stage. There were aggressive retorts and protests as she attempted to gain ground; hands snatched at her clothes and arms, holding her back, assuming she was after the cash. She wasn't. Though not a single soul present had more right to it.

It takes one second, one-hundredth of a second, for a situation to flip, for a crowd to flip, for the mood of an entire event to change course, like the shift of wind in a sail. All those banknotes drifting through the air had flipped the mood. Shoving my way to the edge of the crowd, I began to run, and as I ran I watched how it happened, how the calm, pleasant atmosphere vanished in the blink of an eye and panic swept the crowd, transforming it into a mob. Below the platform, the crush churned; any minute now people would lose their balance and be trampled to death.

Lilou was surrounded by an angry throng, but I hazarded she could take care of herself. With longer legs and a narrower profile, I swung wide, tearing through the sparser edges of the crush, slipping round my opponents like Lionel Messi. I reached the stage well before Lilou, elbowed my way past the volunteer stewards, and began to climb the metal scaffolding. The pipes scorched my hands and it was too hot to breathe, my lungs flattened, frantically straining to absorb oxygen. Nothing could be done about how light-headed I felt; hesitating on the scaffold was not an option if I didn't want to leave the charred skin of my palms behind on the metal.

Above on stage, Arnaud had pulled the cork from his wine bottle and was splashing its contents on the platform at his feet. It pooled around him, and people nearby, sensing something I couldn't yet identify, began backing away. As I reached the edge of the platform I smelled it.

Not wine.

Petrol.

An inkling of Arnaud's plan began to dawn on the people around him and – hesitantly at first, then panicked, scrambling to leave the stage – they crowded the stairs, sliding down scorching poles as he emptied the remains of the petrol on to the priceless painting.

The painting.

He'd turned it to face the crowd, but could they

see what it was? Could they see that it was not some imitation mass-produced copy, some cheap museum shop replica? My heart did something strange in my chest, and I wanted to shout.

Please, Arnaud. Please don't.

Arnaud pulled a cheap plastic lighter out of his pocket and began his final speech. '*C'est à cause du pétrole qu'on en est là,*' he said into the microphone, his voice calm and even. '*It is oil that has brought us to this place. It is oil that will carry us away. I volunteer to represent you as the first conscious martyr of climate change. But,*' he said, '*you can rest assured, I will not be the last.*'

I faced Arnaud, pulled a microphone from its stand, and shouted. A single word. The first that came into my head.

'*ARRÊTE!!*'

Stop. The word boomed out with such force that the entire crowd froze. The unexpected suspension of thousands upon thousands of people below us in

200

the park and on the streets was the loudest silence I had ever heard.

Arnaud blinked into the glaring sun, stunned, as if woken from a particularly compelling dream. Casting about blankly for a second or two, he at last seemed to recognise me and understand the situation.

He paused.

And then flicked the lever on his cigarette lighter.

19

The stage exploded in flame.

Arnaud too.

The Matisse.

The money.

And everyone who was still standing on the platform.

Including me.

It was encouraging to discover that in moments of extreme crisis, the unconscious mind acts without permission of the conscious, and in this case, it took a mere portion of a fraction of a second, maybe less, for me to launch myself at Arnaud, not very cleverly or accurately, but with enough direction and force to hurl us both off the stage.

The last image my retina recorded on the platform was the howling fireball within which the beautiful painting blackened and died.

Afterwards I imagined us tumbling towards earth, poetically, like Icarus (and his mate), wings burning from too close a brush with the sun.

But it didn't feel poetic at the time.

Arnaud and I landed together on top of the crowd, who couldn't avoid us due to the crush. We were cushioned by the people who broke our fall, some of whom no doubt suffered injuries from the impact. We landed as we'd flown through the air, together, in flames. Some anonymous genius had the presence of mind to save our lives by smothering the flames with a banner.

Anonymous genius, if you're reading this, I am eternally grateful to the quickness of your reflexes, and your wit.

The banner read, more appropriately than I could ever have devised, *NOUS BRÛLONS*.

We are burning.

I know this in retrospect only. It made the front page of nearly every major newspaper in the world – at least those that didn't choose the close-up of a multi-million-pound painting disguised as a fireball.

Le Bonheur de Vivre. The joy of life.

20

People in the movies tend to wake up in hospital asking what day it is and there's usually a kindly nurse present to fill in the backstory.

'Well,' she'd say, attaching a blood pressure cuff to the victim's arm, 'you're a very lucky young man indeed, the doctors said if it hadn't been for that brave woman who smothered the flames and dragged you to safety, you'd never have made it out alive. As it was, things were touch and go for a while and we never gave you more than a one-in-ten chance of survival, but against the odds, here you are, awake and alive. How do you feel?'

And against all odds the victim would feel OK,

despite being covered with burns and bruises, and more than a little befuddled, smeared with soot, and with his hair falling over his forehead in a becoming manner.

'Ah, speak of the devil. Here's that brave young woman now,' the nurse would say, pointing. And indeed, here she was in the doorway of his hospital room, impossibly young and attractive, with sparkling grey eyes and a brow furrowed with concern for the young man whose life she'd saved and whose life story was now inextricably linked with hers.

This was not my story.

The person who broke my fall was a middle-aged Frenchman, tall, and a substantially built ninety kilogrammes. As I plummeted flaming to the ground clutching Arnaud, we landed on him. He didn't save our lives on purpose, and would no doubt have much preferred to step out of the way. Thank goodness he was trapped and that he was a big man. I'd have hated to crush a child.

The banner – *NOUS BRÛLONS* – came afterwards. At the time I thought, Oh Christ, everything's gone dark, I must be blind.

With the exception of a faint smell of burning flesh in my nostrils, that's pretty much all I can report.

21

Sometime later I became aware of being pushed into triage on a gurney. '*Côtes cassées*,' said a nurse with a clipboard, as he carefully examined my torso. '*Et brûlures.*'

I struggled to interpret what that meant; something broken, Côte d'Azur ... did I have a broken coast? Côte de boeuf, a broken side of beef – ah, I see, broken ribs. *Brûlure*s was obvious. I was basically a rib roast. Medium rare. I don't remember the removal of my clothes, but perhaps the flames had burned them off.

The nurse followed up with '*Pouvez-vous avaler?*' which was a verb I didn't know and required gesticulation with pills and a glass of water. It turned out that I could swallow, though even that hurt, and a few minutes after swallowing the pills, I began to feel *merveilleusement bien* and was rolled down to X-ray through a meadow of daisies, giant butterflies and whispering fawns. Upon arrival, the radiographers attempted to inflict a great deal more pain upon me by positioning me in unnatural and unpleasant positions beneath the cameras.

But did I mind? Hell, no! I was a tulip.

'*Désolée*,' the radiographer said, sounding not particularly *désolée* at all. Not that it mattered. I loved her.

Drugged to the gills, I was returned to a bed on the ward and my brain began to roam, wondering whether it might be better just to join the French Foreign Legion and skip the explanations that would inevitably be required at home. I wondered how I'd look in the uniform, picturing parallel rows of shiny brass buttons, white cake-box hat, cross-chest strap ending in a cartridge box and red epaulettes.

So cute!

Victims of the demonstration suffering from burns, broken bones, the usual stampede-type injuries filled my ward. We were a mix of protesters and police, a potentially volatile combination, but no one was in the mood for a fight. Especially not me. I wanted to invite them all to a rave. The best party in the world!

And then in a moment of clarity I remembered Arnaud. Where was he? Was he alive? Had he survived the fire?

A sick feeling accompanied my returning memories. They rose one by one to the surface like stunned fish in a pond. A happy sparkly pond.

There was no sign of Arnaud on the ward, and no one seemed to know where or how he was. I, on the other hand, had become a minor celebrity as the person who'd tried to save his life. Word spread that it was my shout that had stopped a hundred thousand people in their tracks, that I'd been the one to tackle

Arnaud, and as word spread, my stock at the hospital soared. A great deal of appreciative murmuring and pointing followed, and then numerous attempts at high-fives, none of which I could return.

'Hey,' said the doctor. 'I saw you on the news. That was an amazing crash-tackle off the stage.'

'That was you?' said the woman in the next bed, peering at me with growing enthusiasm. 'Have you seen the footage?'

She brought it up on her phone and there we were, though you wouldn't necessarily have known it was Arnaud and me, given we were engulfed in flame.

'Wow,' I said, and passed out.

When next I opened my eyes, Lilou was standing beside me with Harrison, who was using the buttons on my electric bed to move me up and down for obscure reasons of his own. He asked if I wanted anything, water or coffee, but I didn't want coffee, I wanted him to stop folding me in half, and even more urgently I wanted more of whatever was in the pills they'd given me a couple of hours earlier, the ones stuffed full of magic psychedelic love dust.

Lilou told me that I had saved Arnaud's life, that he was heavily sedated in a burns unit but would definitely be dead if it hadn't been for me. It wasn't clear what was going to happen to him, either medically or psychiatrically, but his mother was with him and last they'd heard he was scheduled for skin grafts. Poor Arnaud and his dramatic plan to become the first ever French climate-change martyr. Obviously, it was better for him that it hadn't come off, but he must be feeling terribly let down. Which, I supposed, was better than feeling burned to death.

Lilou was relieved that he might at last get the help he needed.

'But what about your money?' It hurt to talk.

She shrugged. 'I'm thinking of it as a bad investment. Some of it burned and some of it went to a bunch of enthusiastic climate demonstrators. Either way I'll never see it again. That's life. I'll know better next time.'

Even in semi-delirium I remembered that her money was, technically speaking, my money. So, kissing it goodbye inspired mixed feelings.

Just then, Lilou whispered very close to my ear, as if reading my thoughts. 'You are,' she said, 'the bravest, most remarkable boy alive.'

I shut my eyes, and instantly found myself in a glorious multicoloured Matisse landscape, a place of colour, sensation and joy. A place, I reminded myself, that no longer existed except in my own mind.

'Am I really?' I asked Lilou, and she smiled at me, a rainbow smile worthy of a hero in a painting.

'I have to go,' Harrison said. 'I have a concert tonight. And anyway, you need to get back to London. Your parents were on the verge of choosing the hymns for your funeral.'

'You've talked to them?'

'Forgive me for disobeying orders,' he said. 'I had to let them know you were alive. You're all over Instagram and the international news as the amazing human torch. I have a handful of proven flaws, but I am not a sadist.'

Although I didn't particularly think Harrison was a sadist, he clearly had unrealised criminal tendencies. I figured the wider family would have to wait and see whether he answered the call to good (the Baroque repertoire) or evil (grand larceny). I put the odds at around 5:2.

'Are they … annoyed?'

'As opposed to pleased as Punch that their only son disappeared on the streets of Paris in a climate emergency and reappeared as the magnificent flying torch, famous on most continents?'

I took that as a yes.

It was good that Harrison had talked to my parents. They wouldn't be happy about my various lapses in judgement but at least they didn't have to fabricate tributes about what a great kid I'd been.

Harrison took his leave, saying it had been incredibly eventful meeting me and requesting that I not return any time soon. He had, it transpired, gone to Arnaud's address to retrieve his oboe, and then to the police to say his oboe had mysteriously reappeared and they, probably accustomed to such changes of heart among quasi-criminal players of wind instruments, had dropped the case.

As it were.

They didn't accuse him of wasting police time with his fake robbery, as (quite wisely) they hadn't wasted any time on it.

And then a mere five hours later the hospital said it was OK for me to go home. I suspect they'd have kept me in longer if they hadn't needed the bed, but Lilou helped by making it clear that I would be discharged into the care of a responsible adult. This was, in my opinion, debatable, but the hospital didn't seem interested in challenging my guardian's credentials.

215

The nurse who signed my release papers gave a series of instructions, including that I must rest, must not get addicted to painkillers, must shower very carefully until the burns healed, must not raise my arms above my waist, and *absolument définitivement* must not play golf for at least six months. What they forgot to tell me was not to laugh, and not to have new hospital friends who couldn't help themselves when it came to saying amusing things to lighten my mood.

L'infirmière seemed doubtful that any representative of the underfunded British National Health Service would be capable of understanding what sort of aftercare my injuries required, but I assured him that I would report exactly what he told me to whatever British doctor I saw next, i.e. rest and don't play golf.

I thought I might leave out the bit about not taking too many opioids, just for now.

Lilou had been paying close attention to her phone

for the last hour, and she leaped up suddenly with the most delighted look on her face. 'IT PASSED!' she shouted. 'The vote passed! Parliament's approved the new oil tax!' And everyone on the ward cheered because, although the world was still burning, at least they were doing what they could to help.

She took me home in a taxi, my hospital gown and paper trousers alerting anyone who saw us that we'd been part of the demo drama. The taxi driver recognised me from the TV news, gave me a thumbs-up, and wouldn't accept Lilou's money for the fare.

Getting in and out of his car was incredibly painful. (If you happen to feel unimpressed by my capacity for bearing pain, try going about your daily life without using any of the muscles that connect to your ribcage.) Nonetheless, I managed to get up to Lilou's place on the first floor by moving at tortoise speed. I don't think I could have managed another step.

She refused to give me more painkillers ('Too

early') but made up for it with a Gruyère-and-spinach omelette, even better than the one in my dreams, which I devoured like an animal, inexpertly using a spoon and my right hand to eat and basically shovelling it into my mouth. Lilou watched, equal parts amused and appalled.

'It's good no one is here to see the table manners you've acquired in France,' she said, shaking her head.

'May I remind you that I haven't eaten in about a week? Also –' I didn't know the words in French so I used English – 'it's wrong to bully the wounded.'

Lilou smiled. 'You are wonderfully courageous.' She paused and looked me straight in the eye. 'Callum, you are altogether extraordinary, and I have been so happy to know you for this very short time.' She'd been speaking to me entirely in French for some time now but made this short speech in English. 'I recognised something exceptional in you that first night in the bar.'

She did? My eyes filled with tears. Who doesn't want to be recognised as exceptional? I don't think I'd ever felt so happy.

She then made me text my father, tell him I'd explain everything later, but that I needed a ticket on the 11:12 Eurostar out of Gare du Nord tomorrow morning and someone to meet me at the station.

'He will know some of your story from watching the news and talking to Harrison,' she said. 'The burning Matisse and the burning Arnaud have made front pages from here to China.'

Oh Lord. Every parent's dream is to turn on the news and see their child fly through the air in flames. There would be questions in the house.

'Take off your clothes,' she told me when I'd sent the text and, resisting the urge to raise an eyebrow (or faint), I slipped the disposable hospital gown off my battered body. She took some pictures of my torso, 'just to remember you by', and scrolled through them on her phone, texting me what she considered to be the best. The ones she sent showed me covered in burns and deep purple and black bruises. Even I was shocked. They looked either gruesome or like badges of honour, depending on your perspective.

'Can you manage a shower?' she asked.

The honest answer was not really.

So she helped me, as no-nonsense as a nurse. The cool spray of the shower made me shiver with pleasure and when I winced away from the feel of it on my burns, she moved it to uninjured areas. All this nakedness might have been a teenage boy's dream come true, but the fact was that everything hurt, a condition that was not optimally sexy and which also spared me certain obvious embarrassments. Once dry, I managed (gingerly) to sit and then lie down on her bed. Not quite the fantasy scenario I'd imagined. But I didn't want anyone to touch me, not even Lilou.

Breeze from her electric fan felt good against my

damp skin, and at last she gave me two painkillers. The butterflies returned, brushing me tenderly with their psychedelic wings. Seconds later, I was out for the count.

22

'*Réveille-toi.*' I heard the words, but was dreaming about the demo, so deeply asleep that I couldn't extricate myself. The dream pulled at me like sucking mud.

Lilou's face came slowly into focus. 'Wake up, Sleeping Beauty. It's eight o'clock. You have a train to catch.'

I opened my eyes and closed them again. 'Don't make me go home.'

She smiled. 'What would my boyfriend say?'

I tried to sit up, which made me cry out with pain. 'You have a boyfriend?'

'*Peut-être.*'

'You don't.'

She shrugged.

Damn, I thought. She might.

Which was fine, as there was no way we could possibly have had sex even if she'd been interested. The doctor hadn't specifically put it on his list of things not to do with broken ribs, but I can say with some certainty that it belonged there.

Still, she was mostly naked and looked very beautiful sitting next to me on the bed, and when you're only seventeen, that's so much more than you can generally hope for.

I reached out to her, but she slipped out of reach and came back a few minutes later with a cup of coffee and a croissant, which also made me sigh with pleasure.

'Thank you, Lilou.'

She crossed her arms and nodded. 'Have your breakfast. Then we send you back to real life.'

I knew real life was on the cards, but the thought

of my former schoolboy existence made me want to cry. 'Maybe I'll come back to Paris to study,' I said, though I hadn't thought any such thought until one second ago. But now I'd said it, maybe I would.

'What a good plan.' She laced her fingers gently in my hair and looked at me. 'Up,' she said. 'We don't have a lot of time. Come, I'll help you.' And she kissed me, a glorious lingering kiss that didn't last nearly long enough but made me giddy with happiness. 'Your phone is charged, and your father has sent through a ticket.'

'How did you know my password?'

'You told me. Though I don't think you were entirely conscious. You would be a very bad spy, Callum.'

The worst. I wondered what else I'd told her while semi-conscious.

'*T'as beaucoup de textes.*'

'Oh God, no.' The thought of answering a thousand texts when even my fingers hurt was not cheering.

'*Allons-y*,' she said, pulling on her own clothes first. I was sorry to see all that beautiful skin disappear, but she still looked radiant.

'Um. I'm not sure Eurostar will let me on in my paper trousers. Health and safety, et cetera.'

'See if these fit.' She handed me a pair of loose cotton trousers and a T-shirt. Not hers, obviously.

'*De ton copain?*' The boyfriend.

She smiled.

None of it mattered now I was leaving. But maybe I would come back. And maybe my French would be better when I did. And maybe I would start to feel at home here. Or anywhere, really. And maybe Lilou would always think of me as a hero.

I dressed carefully, and she helped. No underpants, but I still had my trainers. The one thing that hadn't burned. She tied the laces, kissed both my knees and picked up my backpack, now nearly empty.

'Ready?'

Not really. I wished I could stay here in this little flat with her forever.

We took a taxi for the short ride to the station and she escorted me to the ticket window, spoke to Eurostar about my injuries and arranged for assistance and a wheelchair. Once I'd settled gingerly into the chair, she wheeled me over to a newsagent and turned me to face a bank of French and international papers. A photo of Arnaud and me in flames occupied nearly every front page, though a slightly blurry zoom-shot of the burning Matisse was a close second. Someone with a long lens had managed to grab the painting's last moment, just before the glorious colours turned to ash. Headlines ran from some version of 'Priceless Painting Martyred for Climate Change' to 'British Student Saves Protester from Raging Inferno'.

I looked at the blackened Matisse and looked away.

'Will you let me know what happens to Arnaud?'

I'd known him less than two days but felt invested in his life and worried about his future.

His near-immolation had accomplished exactly what he'd wished for, thankfully without killing him (or me).

Lilou and I embraced as best we could, carefully, with one arm and a great deal of genuine affection.

'Lilou …' I felt suddenly shy.

'Callum?'

'Why did you kidnap me on your motorbike that first night?'

'*Kidnappé?*' She half laughed. It wasn't what she'd expected me to say. 'Well, I had not intended to. But when I drove past, you were standing outside looking so hopeful. Waiting. As if something good might still happen.' She shrugged. 'I fell in love with your hopefulness. *C'était un caprice.*'

A whim. 'OK. Well, thank you,' I said, 'for *la caprice.*'

'Le *caprice*,' she said, rolling her eyes.

'Any sort of caprice.'

She kissed me goodbye, very gently, so as not to cause pain, and hugged me once more on my good side, and then she left. I watched her go, watched her turn back at the bottom of the escalator to wave. I wondered if she really did have a boyfriend.

As my train pulled out of Gare du Nord at 11:12 precisely, I switched on my messages with a sense of resignation. There were six hundred and thirty-five of them.

The first, from Moe, read: WTF MAN! WHAT HAPPENED?

What happened?

Good question, Moe, my friend.

I went AWOL, found my cousin, slept through an oboe concert, met Arnaud and Lilou, was unexpectedly abducted, rode behind a mysterious Parisienne on a motorbike through corners of Paris I never dreamed existed, drank a tisane in the Sixteenth, fell in love with a glorious painting, was chased by the police, went to a sex club, became an accessory to insurance fraud, gave a great deal of money that wasn't mine to a girl I barely knew, hitched a ride on an American tour bus, encountered a stolen oboe, got swept up in a climate demo, silenced a hundred thousand people with a single word, caught fire, saved a man's life, broke some ribs, rode in a French ambulance, spent an afternoon in hospital, appeared on the front pages of news stories around the world, kissed an amazing girl, slept beside her overnight …

How could I tell Moe all of this? Any of it?

How could I tell him I'd fallen in love with a girl and a painting and my life for the first time, fallen in love with adventure, and with France – a completely different France from the one I first met. How could I tell him about the heat, about political action, about Lilou?

I couldn't put all that into words, so for now I said nothing.

23

At St Pancras Station, my parents forgave me for skipping out on the train, but not for worrying them almost to death over forty-eight hours. I apologised as best I could, and subtly emphasised my hunched and battered state, which helped a lot in the sympathy stakes.

'My poor baby,' sniffed my mother, her face drawn with sympathy, as my dad acted out an entire opera based on the brutal execution of the Prodigal Son over her shoulder.

Mum choked out that she was just so grateful I was alive. And Dad eventually admitted that he had, in fact, taken a job in Dubai, but that us kids didn't have to come as it was only a six-month contract.

Remembering what Lilou had said about it being his life and his job, I shrugged, which hurt, and wished him good luck.

I hadn't yet broached the question of the money I'd given away and was just about to bite the bullet and confess when my phone pinged, and when I looked, I saw it was a notification of payment to my account of two thousand euros, deposited by one Mlle Lilou Messaoui.

I texted her back. 'Happy Birthday, my *merveilleuse* Lilou,' I wrote, 'and thank you for le Bonheur de Vivre.'

And then, because she was the reason my summer had turned out thrilling, alarming, risky, sexy, astonishing, glorious, unexpected, heroic and life-changing, I added a heart.

Have you read

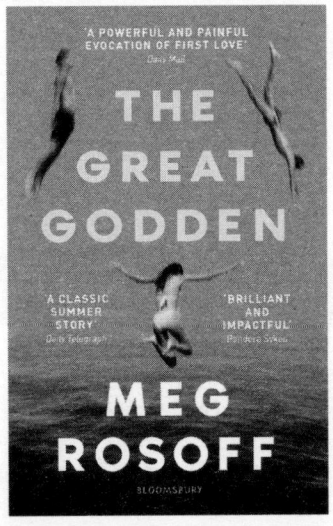

SHORTLISTED FOR THE COSTA BOOK AWARDS

A timeless book that crystallises a moment of
growing up

'A sun-drenched coming-of-age story … seductive
and elegant … The heady nostalgia and sweet ache
of first love and lost innocence recall classics such
as *Bonjour Tristesse*' – *Observer*

AVAILABLE NOW!

And look out for

An alluring coming-of-age tale about the summer
that changes everything

'An irresistible account of female friendship …
Nobody describes the strength, pain and comedy of
being young as elegantly and eloquently as Meg
Rosoff' – Amanda Craig

Turn the page for a sneak peek …

1

Arriving in New York for the first time was like wearing a sign that said CHEAT ME.

Muggers mugged. Junkies jacked up. Pickpockets picked pockets. Flashers flashed, rapists raped and perverts perved. Psycho bag ladies shouted obscenities at miscellaneous crazies. You could get shot just for being in the path of a bullet. AIDS knew where you lived.

Heaps of garbage stank on every corner. Taxis honked, hawkers shouted, brakes screamed. Women jeered, flirted, complained in a barely comprehensible language. *Gedda hell oudda heah! Don' fuckwidme mistah*. The midday sun bounced off ten million glaring surfaces.

Dragging her suitcase out of the station on the hottest day of the year, Beth dripped sweat. Signs made unhelpful suggestions: Seventh Avenue, Eighth. Thirty-first Street. Thirty-third. She didn't dare ask directions for fear of being taken for a fool. Or worse, a tourist.

She stuck out her arm and a taxi swerved. Shoving her suitcase on to the seat, she fell in after it and closed the door.

'Christopher Street,' she gasped, hoping he'd know where that was. And then, just like that, they were off. The sweet smell of decay blew in through the open window mixed with exhaust fumes and melted tar.

Beth sat back in the cab and sighed. *Remember this time and place*, she thought. *New York City, June 1983. This is where it starts.*

Already her life felt like a miracle.

2

'Which corner?' In the mirror the driver waited for an answer, rolled his eyes.

Which corner? She frowned. Why did it matter?

He screeched to a halt. 'Two thirty-five,' he said, shaking his head, thinking (no doubt) he could have charged this girl anything.

She fumbled in her purse, found three dollars, handed it over, threw open the door and fell out on to the melting sidewalk with her bag.

'Keep the change,' she whispered as he sped away.

The lock on the building's front door was broken. Inside, a single bulb illuminated peeling paint and a row of dented metal mailboxes. The heat was unbearable. She hauled her suitcase to the foot of the stairs and began to climb, stopping on each landing to wipe the sweat from her hands.

On the fifth floor she flicked the light switch and recoiled.

A figure sat slumped against the door, glaring. 'It's about fucking time. I've been waiting in this hell-hole all day.'

Beth gaped.

'Open the door, for fuck's sake.' The strange girl snatched Beth's keys. 'I'll do it,' she said, pushing her own suitcase in first. 'Christ what a fucking dump.'

'I'm ...'

'I know who you are. You're Rachel's friend. Bernie. Betsy. Barbie.'

'Beth.'

A dark hall led to a tiny living room (no window) with a door on each side. The kitchen was only big enough for one person, the bathroom too small for a sink. A definite scurrying in her peripheral vision when she turned on the light. Cockroaches.

The apartment came furnished. In the living room, a Chinese scroll hung sideways over a small oatmeal-coloured sofa, like you'd find in a dentist's waiting room. A wooden folding chair and a small glass coffee table completed the suite. The only shelf held a dusty wine bottle covered in drips.

Rachel's sister dumped her bag in the near bedroom and ran the water in the kitchen, waiting unsuccessfully for it to cool. 'I'm Dawn. Tom should be here already. He has the keys.'

Beth hated people referring to strangers as if you should know them. Who was Tom? Her boyfriend? Her cat?

'Oh,' Beth said. 'Thanks for letting me live here.'

'Couldn't afford it without you. Have to find a job. You got one, right?' She looked Beth up and down, as if to say, *If you got a job, I can get ten.*

Beth nodded.

'We've got to do something about this place. I can't live in a fucking slum.'

'Do you mind if ...' Beth edged towards the door.

'Be my guest.'

Beth dragged her bag into the second bedroom. Small double bed, narrow bedside table, chest of drawers. Barely room for a person. Bare bulb overhead.

How could it be so hot?

Across the way, a brick tenement identical to theirs had fire escapes running up and down like zips on a biker jacket. She opened the window and stuck her head out over the street, desperate for air. A muffled clamour rose from below. It was hotter outside than in.

Stripping off her clothes, she fell back on the bare mattress.

Ugh, she thought. *I need a shower*.

The door to Dawn's room was closed when Beth stepped out in a towel. She hurried to the bathroom, stood under the cold shower till her blood cooled, then stood dripping on the wet tile floor. No bath mat, no shower curtain. Water trickled from the ceiling and ran down the walls; the entire apartment had become a rainforest. She was sweating again by the time she reached her bedroom.

Beth made the bed and unpacked into the chest of drawers. A few stray items at the back – green nylon underpants, torn T-shirt, single grey sock – she dumped guiltlessly in the trash.

And that was it. Home.

Lying naked on the bed, she spread the damp towel over her torso. If you didn't move, it wasn't too bad.

As the light slipped away, Beth heard a male voice in the next room. *Must be Tom*, she thought. Not a cat then. She lacked the energy to check. It was too hot to get dressed. Too hot to talk. Definitely too hot to talk to Dawn.

Outside, singing, swearing and shouting rose up in a spew of noise. New York City after dark sounded savage.

She turned off the light and tried to sleep.

3

The next morning, Beth woke early, dressed and went out. The bars on Christopher Street were closed, clientele gone to their beds or someone else's. Ten minutes of wandering led her to The Acropolis, a blue, white and chrome Greek coffee shop. Within seconds she'd been steered to a counter seat, a menu slapped in front of her.

'Coffee?' The waiter held up a pot.

She nodded, grateful. He filled a heavy white mug and slid a metal container of milk in front of her.

Beth ordered the Breakfast Special – two eggs any style, pancakes, hash browns, bacon, sausage and toast. She hadn't eaten since breakfast the day before. Her plate arrived with far too much food, but she ate it all, accepting extra toast and coffee because it was free. The waiters treated her with reassuring indifference.

After breakfast, with no desire to encounter Dawn and Tom, she set off exploring. From the air-conditioned coffee shop, outdoors hit her like a hammer. Not even ten and already creeping up towards a hundred degrees.

She walked and walked. And looked and looked. And walked. And looked. Veered into a pizza joint.

'Please,' she said. 'Could I please have some water …'

The pizza man filled a giant waxed cup with water and ice. He waved when she reached for her wallet. 'I'm not gonna charge you for ice.'

Her hands, thick with heat, dipped into the cup.

For hours, Beth sat in Washington Square watching people come and go. All around her, New

Yorkers in sunglasses, stiletto heels, flip-flops and roller skates flowed from here to there and back again, impervious to weather and everything else.

Eventually she got up and wandered off again through the streets. She stopped at a store advertising air-con and exotic gifts, with hash pipes, ropes of silver jewellery, T-shirts printed with marijuana leaves and books of Indian poetry in the window. Inside it stank of patchouli. She took her time, searching the glass cases as if for something specific, though the salesgirl ignored her. Wreathed in cool air, Beth's eyes glazed over with pleasure. Could she stay here all day?

Her damp clothes began to turn icy.

'You need help?' The girl looked up at last. She was young, hippieish.

Beth pointed to a large black-and-white poster of Debbie Harry looking sideways at the camera. 'How much is that?'

'It's the last one and it's torn. You can have it for a

buck.' Not waiting for assent, the girl pulled it off the wall and rolled it up.

'You want the tacks?'

Beth nodded and exchanged them for a damp dollar bill from her pocket. Indian goat bells tinkled on the door as she left.

For a few seconds the heat outside was bliss.

Box fans formed a pyramid in front of a hardware store. *Get 'Em While They're Hot* said the handwritten sign. She bought one, and a cheap desk lamp.

Back on her block, the party she'd heard the night before was in full swing. It wasn't frightening down here, just giddy and feverish. Men in tight satin micro shorts or jeans and tank tops arrived outside bars where people already gathered to drink, talk, hold hands and kiss. Couples dressed head to toe in leather strolled past oblivious to the heat. She'd never noticed gay people back home; they all must live here.

Beth threw her shoulder at the front door and

flicked on the light. The bulb blew with a flash and she trudged up to 5E in the dark.

Nobody home, much to her relief. Dumping her treasures on the bed, she set up her new lamp. It was better than the ghoulish overhead but nothing could fix the depressing atmosphere of the place. The only cheering feature was a slim bookcase pushed up against the living-room wall, with best-sellers from past years, a few classics, and half a dozen old books with brightly illustrated covers. Some previous tenant had been a reader. She plugged in the fan and switched it to high, then stood on her bed to hang the poster. Tacks slid easily into the flimsy wall.

Beth stepped back. Debbie Harry looked strong. *I will surround myself with strong women*, she thought. *And become like them.*

Stripping down to her T-shirt, she dozed off to the noisy whoosh of the fan, waking early evening in a drugged haze, her sheets damp with sweat, hungry but unwilling to brave the endless stairs. From the corner of her eye she glimpsed scuttling.

Both windows faced the street so there was no chance of a cross-breeze. Beth soaked her T-shirt in cold water and wore it to bed. When she woke at midnight it was bone-dry, so she soaked it once more and went back to sleep, clammy, hot and cold at once.

From deep within a heat-haze dream she heard Dawn and Tom come in.

Saturday night on Christopher Street sounded like an insurrection.

About the Author

Meg Rosoff is a Fellow of the Royal Society of Literature and winner of the Carnegie Medal, the Deutscher Jugendliteraturpreis and the coveted Astrid Lindgren Memorial Award. Meg grew up in a suburb of Boston and moved to London in 1989. She spent fifteen years working in advertising before writing her first novel, *How I Live Now*, which has sold more than one million copies in thirty-six territories. She has written nine young-adult novels, *Jonathan Unleashed* for adults, and a middle-grade series about a dog called McTavish, who rescues a chaotic family. Meg lives in London.